THE BOBBSEY TWINS BOOKS

By Laura Lee Hope

The Bobbsey Twins
- In the Country
- At the Seashore
- At School
- At Snow Lodge
- On a Houseboat
- At Meadow Brook
- At Home
- In a Great City
- On Blueberry Island
- On the Deep Blue Sea
- In Washington
- In the Great West
- At Cedar Camp
- At the County Fair
- Camping Out
- And Baby May
- Keeping House
- At Cloverbank
- At Cherry Corners
- And Their Schoolmates
- Treasure Hunting
- At Spruce Lake
- Wonderful Secret
- At the Circus
- On an Airplane Trip
- Solve a Mystery
- On a Ranch
- In Eskimo Land
- In a Radio Play
- At Windmill Cottage
- At Lighthouse Point
- At Indian Hollow
- At the Ice Carnival
- In the Land of Cotton
- In Echo Valley
- On the Pony Trail
- At Mystery Mansion
- At Sugar Maple Hill
- In Mexico
- Toy Shop
- In Tulip Land
- In Rainbow Valley
- Own Little Railroad
- At Whitesail Harbor
- And the Horseshoe Riddle
- At Big Bear Pond
- On a Bicycle Trip
- Own Little Ferryboat
- At Pilgrim Rock

The cowboy taught the Bobbsey twins how to twirl a lasso

The Bobbsey Twins in the 'reat West

The Bobbsey Twins in the Great West

By

LAURA LEE HOPE

GROSSET & DUNLAP
Publishers *New York*

PRINTED IN THE UNITED STATES OF AMERICA

The Bobbsey Twins in the Great West

CONTENTS

CHAPTER I

THE TRAIN WRECK

"Come on, let's make a snow man!" cried Bert Bobbsey, as he ran about in the white drifts of snow that were piled high in the yard in front of the house.

"That'll be lots of fun!" chimed in Freddie Bobbsey, who was Bert's small brother. "We can make a man, and then throw snowballs at him, and he won't care a bit; will he, Bert?"

"No, I guess a snow man doesn't care how many times you hit him with snowballs," laughed the older boy, as he tried to catch a dog that was leaping about in the drifts, barking for joy. "The more snowballs you throw at a snow man the bigger he gets," said Bert.

"Oh, Bert Bobbsey, he does not!" cried a girl

with dark hair and sparkling brown eyes, as she ran along with a smaller girl holding her red-mittened hand. "A snow man can't grow any bigger! What makes you tell Freddie so?"

"Course a snow man can grow bigger!" declared Bert. "A snowball grows bigger the more you roll it in the snow, doesn't it?"

"Yes," admitted Nan—Nan being the name of the brown-eyed girl, Bert's twin sister. "I know a snowball grows bigger the more you roll it, but you don't roll a snow man!" went on the brown-eyed girl.

"Ho, ho! wouldn't that be funny?" laughed the little girl, whose hand Nan held.

"What would be funny, Flossie?" asked Freddie, and one look at the two smaller Bobbsey children would have told you that they, too, were twins. In fact the four Bobbseys were twins—that is there were two sets of them—Bert and Nan, and Flossie and Freddie. "What would be funny?" Freddie wanted to know. "Tell me! I want to laugh."

"Yes, you generally do want to laugh, little fireman!" and Bert Bobbsey laughed himself, as he gave his small brother the pet name that Daddy Bobbsey had thought up some time ago. "But, as Flossie says, it would be funny to see a snow man rolling around in the drifts to make himself bigger," went on Bert.

"But you said he'd get bigger if we threw snowballs at him," insisted Nan.

"And he will," went on Bert. "You see, a snowball gets bigger when you roll it around the yard, because more snow keeps sticking to it all the while. And if we make a snow man and then throw little snowballs at him, these snowballs will stick to him and he'll grow bigger, won't he?"

"Oh, I didn't know you meant *that* way!" and now Nan, herself, began to laugh. Of course Flossie and Freddie joined in, though I am not sure that they knew what the joke was all about, but they were having fun in the snow and that was all they cared for.

It was a fine snow storm, at least for the Bobbsey twins and the other children of Lakeport. It was not too cold, and the white flakes had come down so fast that there was now enough snow to make many snow men and snowballs, and leave plenty for coasting down hill.

The Bobbsey twins had hurried out to play in the snow as soon as they got home from school, and now they were having fine fun. Snap, their dog, was playing with them, leaping about in the drifts, diving through them, as the Bobbsey twins had seen swimmers dive through waves down at the seashore and Snap would come out on the other side of the drift all covered with white flakes, as though he were a snow dog.

Dear old Dinah, the fat, jolly, good-natured colored cook, who had been with the Bobbseys many years, stood at the window looking at the children having fun in the snow.

"Why doesn't yo' go out an' jine 'em?" she asked, as she looked at a sleek cat that was curled up asleep near the stove. "Why doesn't yo' go out in de snow? Dat's whut I asks yo', Snoop," went on Dinah. "Dar dey is—Flossie an' Freddie an' Nan an' Bert. An' Snap's out wif 'em, too. Why don't yo' go out an' jine de party?"

But Snoop seemed to like it better by the

warm fire. He didn't want to "jine" any party, as Dinah called it. Snoop didn't like snow or water.

"Well, shall we make a snow man?" asked Bert, as he raced about with Snap, making the dog chase after sticks which would become buried deep under the snow, where Snap had to dig them out. But the dog liked this.

"Let's make a snow house. I think that would be more fun," said Nan.

"Oh, yes, and I can get my doll, and we can have a play party in the snow house," cried Flossie.

"Can't we take the snow man into the snow house?" Freddie wanted to know. "That'll be more fun than dolls. And we can make believe the snow house gets on fire, and I'll be a fireman and put it out. Oh, let's play that!" he cried, his eyes shining in fun.

"Yes, anything like playing fireman suits *you*," returned Bert. "But it would be pretty hard even to *pretend* a snow house was burning. Snow can't catch fire, Freddie!"

"Well, we could make believe!" said the little fellow. "Anyhow, I'm going to start to make a snow man, and you can make the snow house."

"And I'll get my doll!" added Flossie, starting toward the house, her little fat legs and feet making holes in the snow drifts as she tried to hurry along.

"Wait, I'll carry you," offered Nan. "You're getting so fat, little fairy, that you'll look like a snow man yourself, if you keep on."

"Are snow mans always fat?" asked Flossie.

"They always seem to be," Nan said, as she lifted up her little sister in her arms. Snap, the dog, came flurrying through the snow after them. "My, I can hardly carry you!" panted Nan, for Flossie was indeed growing fast, and was heavy.

However, Nan managed to carry Flossie over to a path Mr. Bobbsey had told Sam, who was Dinah's husband, to shovel through the snow that morning. It was easier for Flossie to walk on the shoveled path, so Nan put her down.

The two girls went into the house, Flossie to get her doll, while Nan went to the kitchen and said something to Dinah, the fat, jolly cook.

"Suah, I gibs 'em to yo'!" exclaimed Dinah,

laughing all over at Nan's question. "I'll *put* 'em in a bag, so's yo'all won't spill 'em!"

And when Flossie was ready to go out again with her doll, Nan went with her, carrying a bag, at which Snap sniffed hungrily.

"What you got?" asked the little girl.

"Oh, you'll see pretty soon," Nan answered.

"Is it a secret?" Flossie kept on teasing.

"Sort of secret," Nan answered.

When the two girls reached the place where they had left the two boys, Bert was beginning to make a snow house and Freddie was rolling a snowball as the start of a snow man. You know how they are made; a small snowball for the man's head, and a larger one for his body, with legs underneath. Freddie hoped Bert would help him when it came to the big snowball part of it.

"Is the snow house ready?" asked Flossie, who had gone in especially to get her doll, so she might have a "play party."

"Oh, no, it takes a good while to make a snow house," Bert said. "I don't believe I'll get it done before night if you don't help me."

"I'll help," offered Flossie. "Can I make the chimbley?"

"They don't have chimbleys on a snow house!" declared Freddie, pausing in his rolling of the snowball. "They don't have chimbleys on snow houses, 'cause they don't have fires in 'em; do they Bert?"

"That's right, Freddie," agreed the older boy. "But maybe, if Flossie wants it, we could put a make-believe chimney on the snow house."

"Oh, I do want it—awful much!" cried Flossie. "Come on, Nan, you help Bert make the snow house, and then we can all play in it."

"And you've got to let my snow man come in!" cried Freddie.

"Yes, we'll let him come in if you don't make him too big," agreed Bert, with a laugh.

Bert and Nan, the older Bobbsey twins, generally did what they could to please Flossie and Freddie, who sometimes wanted their own way too much.

"I guess I'll help make the snow house first," went on Freddie, walking away from the snowball he had partly rolled. "After that I'll make the man. It's better to make the house first, and then I'll know how big I can make the man."

"Yes, that would be a good idea, little fireman!" returned Bert, with a laugh and a look at Nan. And then Bert caught sight of the bag in his sister's hand—the bag around which Snap was sniffing so hungrily.

"What have you, Nan?" asked Bert, pausing in the midst of shoveling snow in a heap for the start of the snow house.

"Oh—something!" and Nan smiled.

"Something good?" Bert went on.

"I guess they're good," Nan said, smiling. "I haven't tasted 'em yet, but Dinah nearly always makes good cookies!"

"Oh, have you got some of Dinah's cookies?" cried Bert, dropping the shovel, and running toward Nan. "Give me some! Please!"

"I want some, too!" cried Flossie.

"So do I!" chimed in Freddie.

Snap didn't say anything, but from the way he barked and leaped about I am sure he, too, wanted some of the cookies.

"Dinah gave me enough for all of us," said Nan, as she opened the bag. "Yes, and there's a broken piece off one that you can have," she went on to Snap, the dog.

Beginning with Flossie, then handing one to Freddie, next passing a cookie to Bert and helping herself last, as was polite, Nan gave out the cookies. Forgotten, now, were snow houses, snow men, snowballs, and even Flossie's doll. The Bobbsey twins were eating Dinah's cookies.

They had each begun on the second helping, when suddenly a loud crash sounded, which seemed to come from the direction of the railroad tracks which ran not far from the Bobbsey home. The crash was followed by loud shouting.

"I wonder what that was?" cried Bert.

"Sounded like thunder," returned Nan.

"Let's go and see," said Bert.

Just as they were starting from the yard, Charley Mason, a boy who lived farther up the street, on the hill, came running along.

"Oh, you ought to see it!" he cried, his eyes big with wonder.

"See what?" asked Bert.

"Smash-up on the railroad, down in the

rocky cut!" answered Charlie. "Two engines smashed together, and the cars are all busted! I saw it from the top of the hill! I'm going down! Come on!"

CHAPTER II

THE QUEER OLD MAN

The first impulse of Bert and Nan Bobbsey was, of course, to rush out of the yard and go with Charley Mason to see the train wreck. And, naturally, as soon as Bert and Nan began to run, Flossie and Freddie, forgetting snow men, snow houses, and even Dinah's cookies, started after their older brother and sister.

"Go on back!" cried Bert to the two smaller children. "You can't come with us!"

"We want to see the wreck!" declared Freddie. "Maybe it's on fire, an' if I'm goin' to be a fireman I must see fires!"

He always declared he was going to be a fireman when he grew up, and he was eager to see the engines every time they went out in answer to an alarm of fire.

"Come on, Bert, if you're coming!" called

Charley Mason, from the street in front of the Bobbsey home. "It's a terrible wreck—cars off the track—engines all smashed up—everything!"

"Here, Nan, you take Flossie and Freddie into the house! I'm going with Charley!" said Bert.

"I want to see the wreck, too!" objected Nan. "You go into the house, Freddie, and I'll bring you a lollypop when I come back," she added.

"Don't want a lollypop! I want to see the busted engines!" declared Freddie almost ready to cry.

"So do I!" chimed in Flossie. She generally did want to see the same things Freddie saw.

"Oh, dear! what shall we do?" exclaimed Nan.

Just then, from the door, Mrs. Bobbsey called:

"Children, children, what's the matter? What was that loud noise that seemed to shake the house?"

"It's a train wreck and I want to go down

with Charley Mason to see it!" answered Bert. "But Flossie and Freddie want to come, and they're too little and—and—"

Then Flossie and Freddie began to talk, and so did Nan and so did Charley, and there was so much talking that I will wait a few minutes for every one to get quiet, and then go on with the story.

And, while I am waiting, I will tell my new readers something about the Bobbsey twins as they have been written about in the books that come before this one in the series.

The four children lived in the eastern city of Lakeport, at the head of Lake Metoka. Mr. Bobbsey was in the lumber business, and boats on the lake in summer and trains on the railroad in winter brought piles of boards to his yard.

"The Bobbsey Twins" is the name of the first book of this series, and in it you may read of the fun Bert and Nan and Flossie and Freddie had together, playing with Charley Mason, Danny Rugg, Nellie Parks and other children of the neighborhood. Sometimes the children had little quarrels, as all boys and girls do, and, once in a while, Bert and Nan would be "mad at" Charley Mason or Danny Rugg. But they soon became friends again, and had jolly times together. Just at present Charley and Bert were on good terms.

The second book is called "The Bobbsey Twins in the Country," and those who have read it remember the summer spent on the farm of Uncle Daniel Bobbsey and his wife Sarah, who lived at Meadow Brook.

Another uncle, named William Minturn, a brother-in-law of Mrs. Bobbsey's, lived at Ocean Cliff; and in the third book, called "The Bobbsey Twins at the Seashore," you may learn of the good times Bert and the others had playing on the beach and having adventures.

After that the Bobbsey twins went to school, and they spent part of a winter at Snow Lodge. Some time later they made a trip on a houseboat, and stopped again at Meadow Brook. The next adventures of the children took place at home, and from there they went to a great city where many wonderful things happened. Blueberry Island was as nice a place as the name sounds, and Bert, Nan, Flossie, and Freddie never forgot the fun they had there. It was almost as exciting as when they traveled on the deep, blue sea. But you can imagine how happy the Bobbsey twins were when their father told them he was going to take them to Washington!

The book about the Washington trip, telling of the mystery of Miss Pompret's china, comes just before the one you are now reading, and it was on their return from that capital city that the children were having fun in the snow.

Christmas had come and gone, bringing much happiness, and it was because they had discovered some of Miss Pompret's missing china in a very strange way that the Bobbsey twins had a much nicer Christmas than usual.

After the holidays winter set in hard and fast, but of course it could not last forever, and there were some who said this snow storm, which gave the Bobbsey twins such a fine chance to have fun, would be the last of the season.

It was, as I have told you, while Bert, Nan, Flossie, and Freddie were making a snow house and a snow man that they had heard the loud crash and Charley Mason had called out about the wreck.

"Has there really been an accident?" asked Mrs. Bobbsey, when the talk had somewhat quieted down.

"Oh, yes'm!" exclaimed Charley. "From my house up on the hill I can look right down into the railroad cut. I was out feeding my dog, and I heard the noise and I looked and I saw the two engines all smashed together and cars off the track and a lot of people running around and—and—everything!"

Charley had to stop to catch his breath.

Mrs. Bobbsey looked down the street and saw a number of men and women and some girls and boys hurrying to the railroad tracks.

"We want to go to see it!" begged Bert.

"And we want to go, too!" pleaded Freddie.

Sam Johnson, the husband of Dinah, the cook, came around the corner of the house.

"There's somethin' must 'a' happened down by the railroad," he said to Mrs. Bobbsey.

"Yes, it's a wreck," she answered. "The

children want to go, but I can't have them going alone. You may take them down, Sam, but if it is too bad—you know what I mean, too many people hurt—bring them right back."

"Yassum, I'll do that there!" agreed Sam, glad himself to get the chance to see what all the excitement was about. "Come along, chil-luns!" he added, with a smile.

"Oh, now we can go!" cried Flossie, as she raced over and took one of Sam's hands. "Now we can go!"

"Yep! Sam'll take care of us. Won't you, Sam?" asked Freddie as he took the other hand. "And if there's a fire I can go near the firemen, can't I?" he begged.

"We'll see," said the colored man, with a nod to Mrs. Bobbsey to show that he understood how to look after the smaller twins.

"Come on!" cried Charley. "I want to see that wreck!"

"So do I!" added Bert, as he hurried on ahead with Nan and Charley. Sam, leading Flossie and Freddie by the hands, followed more slowly out into the street, where the side-walks had been cleared of snow so the walking was easier. Snap, the dog, tried to follow, but fearing that he might get hurt, Bert drove him back.

The railroad ran at the foot of the street on which the Bobbsey house stood. The street went downhill to the tracks, and the railroad passed through what Charley had called a "cut."

That is, a cut had been made through the side of the hill so the tracks would be as nearly level as possible. Sometimes, when a hill is too high the railroad has to go through it in a tunnel. And a "cut" is a tunnel with the top taken off.

As Bert, Nan, and the others hurried along the street they saw many other persons hastening in the direction of the wreck. In a cutter, drawn by a horse that had a string of jingling bells on, Dr. Brown passed, waving to the Bobbsey twins.

"I guess there must be somebody hurt, or Dr. Brown wouldn't be going," said Charley Mason.

"I guess so," agreed Bert. "I never saw a big wreck."

"Well, this is a big one!" cried Charley. "I saw the two engines all smashed up."

A little later the Bobbsey twins, in charge of Sam, came to the edge of the cut. They could look down to the railroad tracks and see the wreck. Surely enough, two trains had come together, one engine smashing into the other. Both trains were on the same track, and had been going in opposite directions. There was a curve in the cut, and neither engineer had seen the other train coming until it was too late to stop.

"Why—why, they just bunketed right together, didn't they?" cried Freddie. "They just bunketed right together, like my express wagon when it ran into Henry Watson's push-o-mobile the other day."

"That's just what happened," said Bert.

For a moment the Bobbsey twins stood and looked down at the wreck. Just as Charley had said, the two engines were smashed and there were some cars knocked off the track. But the wreck was not as bad as it had seemed at first, and I am glad to say no one was killed, though a number of people were hurt.

The Bobbsey twins could see these persons, who had been passengers on one or the other of the trains, moving about down in the railroad cut. Some of them did not seem to know just what had happened. The accident had so frightened them that they were in a daze.

Trainmen, policemen, and even some firemen, were helping the injured persons away from the wreck. There had been no fire, and, much as Freddie liked to see the engines, he was glad there was no blaze to make matters worse for the poor people who were hurt.

"Dat suah is a smash!" declared Sam, as he stood on the bank, holding the hands of Freddie and Flossie. "Dey suah did bump togedder lickity-smash!"

"Let's go down closer!" suggested Charley Mason.

Bert looked at Sam, as if asking if this might be done.

"No, indeedy!" exclaimed the faithful colored man. "Yo'all jest stay right yeah! Yo'all's ma tole me to look after yo', an' I'se gwine to do it! Yo'all kin see whut dey is to see right yeah! If you goes any closter one ob dem bullgines might blow up!"

"I don't want to be blowed up; do I, Sam?" put in Flossie.

"No, indeedy!" he answered.

"Well, I'm going down!" declared Charley.

And, not having any one with him to make him mind, he slid down the snow-covered bank to the tracks, where there was quite a large crowd now gathered.

The railroad men were starting to work to get the wreck off the tracks, so other trains might pass. The injured persons were being cared for by Dr. Brown and others, and the worst of the wreck seemed over. Still there was much for the Bobbsey twins to look at.

Flossie and Freddie kept tight hold of Sam's hand, and Bert and Nan stood a little way off, gazing down into the cut. As the Bobbsey twins stood there they saw, climbing up a narrow foot-path on the side of the railroad hill, a queer old man. He was dressed somewhat as the children had seen Uncle Daniel Bobbsey dress on a cold day at the farm, with a red scarf about his neck. And this man was carrying his hat in one hand while in the other he held a banana half pealed and eaten.

The queer man seemed very much frightened, and he was hurrying up the hill path as though trying to run away from something. Bert had just time to see that there was a cut on the man's head, which was bleeding, when, all at once, the queer character cried:

"There! I forgot my satchel! I thought this was it!" and he looked at the banana he was carrying. He turned, as though to hurry back down toward the wreck, and then he slipped and fell in the snow.

"Mah goodness!" cried Sam, as he dropped the hands of the smaller Bobbsey twins and sprang toward the man. "You's gwine to slide right down on de tracks ag'in ef you don't be keerful!" And Sam caught the queer man just in time.

CHAPTER III

MR. BOBBSEY REMEMBERS

THE Bobbsey twins at first did not know what to think of the queer man who had fallen down in the snow just as he reached the top of the hill, at the bottom of which was the train wreck. But when Bert noticed the bleeding cut on the head he guessed what had happened.

"I guess he was one of the passengers, and got hurt," said the boy to Nan.

"I guess so, too," she said.

Flossie and Freddie, not having Sam's hand to take hold of now, were holding each other's and watching the colored man help the stranger.

"Hold on now! Jest take it easy!" advised Sam, in a soothing voice. "Yo's gwine to feel better soon. Is you much hurted?"

The man seemed more dazed than ever. He

put his hand to his head, letting go of the banana he had been holding, and when he saw that his fingers were red, because they had touched the bloody cut, he exclaimed:

"Oh, now I remember what happened! I was in the train wreck!"

"That's right! I guess you was," said Sam. "You come up de hill from down by de railroad tracks, an' you done slipped back down ag'in almost! I jest caught you in time!"

"Thank you," said the man. "I really didn't know what I was doing. All I wanted to do was to get away from the wreck, and I took the first path I saw. I must have got out of breath, for when I reached the top of the hill I couldn't go any more, and I just slipped down."

"I saw you!" exclaimed Sam. "Maybe dat whack you got on top ob yo' haid makes you feel funny."

"I rather think it does," said the man. "But I'm feeling better now. When the crash came I jumped out of my seat—as soon as I could get up after being knocked down—and rushed out of the car. I must have been wandering around for some time. Then I saw this path leading up the hill and I took it."

"Why didn't you put your hat on?" asked Bert, who, with the other Bobbsey twins, had been looking closely at the stranger.

"My hat? That's so, I did forget to put it on," he said, and, for the first time, he seemed to remember that he was carrying his hat in his hand.

"You might catch cold," remarked Nan.

"That's right, little girl—so I might," he said, and he smiled at her. He had a kind smile, had the man, though his face looked weary and sad.

"Did you get much hurt in the wreck?" asked Bert.

"No, I think not," was the answer, and again he put his hand to his head. "It's only a cut, I'm thankful to say. I'll be all right in a little while. I'll hold a little snow to it. That will wash the blood off, as well as water would."

With Sam's help, he now managed to stand up. The colored man took up a handful of snow and gave it to the stranger, who held it to the cut on his head. The cold snow seemed to make him feel better, and when he had wiped away the blood he put on his hat, shook the snow from his overcoat, and looked at the banana which he had dropped in a drift.

"Well, I do declare!" cried the stranger.

"What's de mattah?" asked Sam.

"Why, all the while I thought that banana was my satchel," was the answer. "I was eating it when the crash came—eating the banana I mean, not my satchel," and he smiled at Bert and Nan, who smiled back at this little joke. Flossie and Freddie stood there looking on.

"I was sitting in my seat, eating this banana," went on the man, "when, all of a sudden, there was a terrible crash, and I was so shaken up, together with a lot of other passengers, that I fell out of my seat. That's how my head was cut, I suppose. I thought I was grabbing up my satchel, so I could run out and be safe, but I must have kept hold of the banana instead.

"I know I got my hat down from the rack overhead, where I had put it, and then out I rushed. My! it was a terrible sight, though I heard it said that nobody was killed, and I'm glad of that. But it was a terrific crash, and it made me feel dizzy. I evidently didn't know what I was doing."

"I should think so, sah!" exclaimed Sam with a smile. "When a body takes a banana for a satchel he's jest natchully out ob his mind, I say!"

"I didn't seem to come to myself until I got up here on top of the hill," went on the man. "But I'm feeling better now. I'm not really hurt at all, except this cut on my head, and that's only a scratch. I'm going down and get my satchel. I can see the car I was in. It isn't smashed at all. I'll go for my valise."

"I'll go with you," offered Sam. "You chilluns stay heah till I come back," he went on. "Don't move away. I got to he'p dis gen'man find his baggage."

"It will be a great help to me," said the man. "I might get dizzy again and fall. It's rather steep going down that hill. Will the children be all right if you leave them?"

"Yes, we'll stay right here," promised Nan.

"And we'll look after Flossie and Freddie," added Bert.

With this promise, Sam thought it would be all right to go down to the wreck and help the stranger look for the valise he had left near his seat in the car. While the two men were gone, the colored servant helping the other, the Bobbsey twins watched the railroad men starting to clear away the wreck. A big derrick had been brought up on another train, and with this the engines and cars that had left the tracks could be lifted back on to them.

In a short time Sam came back with the man, and the colored helper at the Bobbsey home was carrying a large valise.

"We found it all right," said the stranger. "It was right near my seat. I might have stayed there, but I was so excited I didn't know what I was doing. What place is this, anyhow?"

"This is Lakeport," answered Bert. "The station's down the track a little way. Your train hadn't got to it yet."

"No, the other train got in the way," said the man, with a smile. "Well, accidents will happen, I suppose. So this is Lakeport! Well, this is the very place I was coming to, but I didn't expect to reach it amid so much excitement."

"You were coming here?" repeated Nan.

"To Lakeport, yes. I want to find a Mr. Richard Bobbsey. Maybe you children can tell me where he lives."

The Bobbsey twins looked so surprised on hearing this that the man gazed at them in astonishment.

"Do you know Mr. Bobbsey?" he asked. "I hope he hasn't moved away from here. I want to see him most particularly. Do you know him?"

"Does dey *know* him!" exclaimed Sam, his eyes opening wide. "Does dey *know* him? Well I should say dey *does!*"

"He's our father!" exclaimed Nan and Bert together.

"Mr. Bobbsey your father! Well, I do declare!" cried the strange man, and he smiled at the children. They were beginning to like him very much. "Just think of that now!" he went on. "My railroad train gets in a wreck right near Lakeport, where I want to get off, and first I know I run into Mr. Bobbsey's children! Well, well! To think of that!"

"Here comes daddy now!" cried Flossie, pointing to a figure walking over the snow toward them.

"Oh, Daddy, I saw the train wreck!" yelled Freddie. "And I saw the firemans, I did, but they didn't have any engines, and I—I—I saw—" But Freddie was too much out of breath from running to meet his father to tell any more just then.

It was indeed Mr. Bobbsey who had come along just then. He had come home earlier than usual from the lumberyard office, and his wife had told him that the children had gone down the street with Sam to look at the railroad wreck.

"I'll go down and bring them back," said Mr. Bobbsey. "I heard about the wreck. It isn't as bad as at first they thought it was. No one was killed."

"I'm glad of that," replied his wife. "I told Sam to bring the children back if it was too bad."

So it had come about that Mr. Bobbsey reached the top of the cut, down in which the railroad wreck was, just as the strange man was asking the Bobbsey children about their father.

"Well, little fireman and little fat fairy," asked Mr. Bobbsey of Flossie and Freddie, "did you see all there was to see?"

"I saw the engines all smashed together," answered Flossie.

"And I saw a fireman help get a lady out of a car," added Freddie.

"Is this Mr. Bobbsey?" asked the voice of the man, as he stepped forward and stood near the children's father.

"Yes, that is my name," was the answer. "Did you wish to see me?"

"I came all the way to Lakeport for that," the stranger went on; "but I didn't mean to come in just this exciting way."

"Were you in the wreck?" asked Mr. Bobbsey.

"Oh, yes, he was in it, and he thought a banana was his satchel!" exclaimed Flossie. "Wasn't that funny, Daddy?"

Mr. Bobbsey did not quite know what to make of this.

"Your little girl is quite right," said the man. "I was so excited, from being in the wreck, where I got a cut on the head, that I rushed from the car carrying a banana instead of my valise.

"However, I'm all right now, and Sam here, as the children call him, was good enough to help me get back my satchel," went on the man. "I was just telling the children that I came here to find Mr. Bobbsey, when, to my great surprise, they let me know that he is their father, and along you came."

"Yes, these are my youngsters," said Mr. Bobbsey, smiling at Bert and Nan and Flossie and Freddie. "Sam Johnson helps us look after them, and his wife, Dinah, cooks for us. But what did you want to see me about?" and he looked at the man.

"Don't you remember me?" came the question.

Mr. Bobbsey looked more closely at the stranger. He did not recognize him.

"Hickson is my name," said the man.

"Hiram Hickson. I used to know you when—"

"Oh, now I remember! Now I know you!" cried Mr. Bobbsey. "Hiram Hickson! Of course! I remember you well now! Well, well! This is a surprise! How did you come—"

But just then a loud shouting in the railroad cut below caused Mr. Bobbsey to stop speaking.

"Look out! Look out!" came the cry, and people began rushing away from the cars, some of which were almost overturned, while others were completely on their side. "Look out!" cried the warning voice again.

CHAPTER IV

THE OLD MAN'S STORY

MR. BOBBSEY caught Flossie and Freddie up in his arms and started to run with them. At the same time Sam Johnson pulled Nan to one side, catching hold of her hand, and the strange man, who had said he was Hiram Hickson, took hold of Bert.

"We'd better get out of harm's way!" said Mr. Hickson.

As the Bobbsey twins were thus hurried out of any possible danger the two older children looked back over their shoulders, down to where the railroad wreck was strewed about along the tracks. They saw the railroad men and other persons running away after the warning shout had been given, and Bert and Nan wondered what was going to happen.

They saw a big puff of steam shoot out from one ot the engines that was partly overturned, and then came a loud noise, as of an explosion.

A few moments later, however, the cloud of steam was blown away by the wind, the noise stopped, and the people no longer ran away.

"I guess the danger is over," said Mr. Bobbsey, as he stopped and set Flossie and Freddie down on the ground a little way back from the edge of the cliff, from which they had been looking at the train wreck. "In fact," went on Mr. Bobbsey, "I don't believe we would have been hurt if we had stayed where we were. But when I heard that shouting I didn't know what was going to happen."

"That's right," returned Mr. Hickson, who had let go of Bert. "You never know what is going to happen in a railroad wreck. I didn't have any idea, when I was riding so easily in my seat, that, a minute later, I'd be thrown out with my head cut and a banana in my hand."

"What happened down there, Daddy?" asked Nan.

"There must have been a blow-out, or an explosion, in the locomotive," answered Mr. Bobbsey. "The fire got too hot after the wreck, and the steam burst out at one side of the boiler. But no one seems to be hurt, and I'm glad of that. The wreck was bad enough."

The railroad men and others who had run out of danger when some one, who saw the boiler about to explode, had given the warning, now came back. They started again to clear the tracks so that waiting trains could pass.

"Well, I don't believe there's much more to see," said Mr. Bobbsey. "We'd better be getting back home, children, or your mother will worry about you."

"Can't I stay and see the firemen just a little longer?" begged Freddie.

"I don't believe they are going to do much more," answered his father. "Their work is nearly done. All the people who were hurt have been taken away."

This was true. The scene of the wreck was now being cleared, and in a little while the damaged engine and cars would be hauled away to the shops to be mended.

"Did you get everything belonging to you, Mr. Hickson?" asked Mr. Bobbsey of the man who had been slightly hurt in the wreck.

"Yes, I have my satchel," he answered. "And as I was going to get out at the Lakeport station I'm right at the place where I was going, even if there had been no wreck."

"And so you were coming to see me, were you?" asked Mr. Bobbsey. "Well, I don't know what your plans are, but I would be very glad to have you come to supper with me."

"Maybe your wife mightn't like it," said Mr. Hickson. "She might not be ready for company, and I'd better tell you that I'm quite hungry."

"So'm I!" exclaimed Freddie. "I'm hungry, and I eat a lot. But Dinah—she's our cook—has lots to eat in her kitchen!"

"Well, then maybe she'd have enough for me," replied Mr. Hickson, with a laugh. "If you're sure it won't put your wife out I'll come," he said to Mr. Bobbsey. "I want to see you, anyhow, and have a talk with you. I want to ask your advice."

"Very well, come along, then," returned the children's father.

"We can talk after supper," went on Mr.

Bobbsey, as the little party walked along the Lakeport street away from the railroad wreck. "That is, if you feel able, Mr. Hickson."

"Oh, I'm beginning to feel all right again," said Mr. Hickson. "I was pretty well shaken up and knocked around when the cars stopped so suddenly, and I was a bit dazed, so I didn't know what I was doing—taking a banana for my satchel, for instance!" And he smiled at Flossie and Freddie, who laughed as they remembered how queer this had seemed to them.

"Yes, I'm all right now, Dick," went on the old man, and Bert and Nan wondered how it was that this stranger called their father by the name their mother used in speaking to her husband.

Mr. Bobbsey saw that Bert and Nan were wondering about this, and he explained by saying that he and Mr. Hickson had known each other for many years.

"We used to know one another," said Mr. Bobbsey to his children. "But it's been a good many years since I have seen him."

"Yes, it has been a good many years," said Mr. Hickson, in rather a sad voice. "And they haven't been altogether happy years fo, me, either; I can tell you that, Dick."

"I'm sorry to hear you say so," replied Mr. Bobbsey.

"Were you in lots of railroad wrecks, and did the firemans have to come and get you out?" asked Freddie. To him railroad wrecks seemed very bad things, indeed, though having the firemen come was something he always liked to watch.

"No, this is the only railroad wreck I have ever been in," said Mr. Hickson. "I don't want to be in another, either. No, my bad luck didn't have anything to do with wrecks or firemen. I'll tell you my story after supper," he said to Mr. Bobbsey.

"Will you tell us a story, too?" begged Flossie.

"I'm afraid my kind of story isn't the kind you want to hear," said the man, smiling rather sadly.

"Daddy will tell you a story, little fat fairy!" said Mr. Bobbsey as he gently pinched the chubby cheek of his little girl. "I'll tell you and my little fireman a story after supper."

Flossie and Freddie clapped their hands and danced along the sidewalk in glee at hearing this.

The little party was soon at the Bobbsey home, and you can imagine how surprised Mrs. Bobbsey was when she saw, not only her husband, the children, and Sam coming in the gate, but a strange man. She must have shown the surprise she felt, for Mr. Bobbsey said:

"Mary, you remember Hiram Hickson, don't you? He and I used to know each other when I was a boy in Cedarville."

"Why, of course I remember you!" said the children's mother. "Though I don't know that I should have known you if I had met you in the street."

"No, I've changed a lot, I suppose," said the old man.

"And you have been in the wreck! You are hurt!" exclaimed Mrs. Bobbsey. "Shall I get a doctor?"

"Oh, I'm not hurt anything to speak of," said the man. "Just shaken up a bit and scratched. I'll be all right once I get a cup of tea."

After supper Flossie and Freddie, as had been promised, were taken up on their father's lap, and they listened to one of daddy's wonderful make-believe stories.

"Please put a fairy in it!" Flossie had begged.

"And I want a fireman in it!" exclaimed Freddie.

"Very well then, I'll tell about a fairy fireman who used to put out fires by squirting magical water on them from a morning glory flower," said Mr. Bobbsey.

This pleased both the little children, and when they had listened to the very end, with eyes that were almost closed in sleep, they were taken off to bed.

"Now, if you'll come with me to the library I'll let you tell me your story," said Mr. Bobbsey to Hiram Hickson.

Bert and Nan, who did not have to go to bed as early as did Flossie and Freddie, rather hoped they might sit up and hear the queer man's story. But in this they were disappointed.

However, Mr. Bobbsey let them hear, the

next morning, the reason why Mr. Hickson had traveled to Lakeport.

"He really was coming to see me," said Mr. Bobbsey. "He wants work, he says, and, as he knows something of the lumber trade and as he knew I had a lumberyard, he came to me."

"But hasn't he any folks of his own?" asked Mrs. Bobbsey who, like the children, was listening to her husband.

"He has two sons, but he doesn't know where they are," answered Mr. Bobbsey.

"Did they get hurt in railroad wrecks?" asked Freddie.

"No, I don't believe so," replied his father. "It is rather a sad story. Hiram Hickson is a strange man. He is kind, but he is queer, and once, many years ago, while his two boys were living with him, there was a quarrel. Mr. Hickson says, now, that it was his fault. Anyhow, his two boys ran away, and he has never seen them since."

"Doesn't he know where they are?" asked Bert.

"No, he hasn't the least idea. At first he

didn't try to find them, for he was angry with them, and he thinks they were angry with him. But, as the years passed, and he felt that he had not done exactly right toward his boys, he began to wish he could find them.

"But he could not, though he wrote to many places. His wife was dead, and he was left all alone in the world. He has a little money, but not much, and, as he is strong and healthy, he felt that he wanted to go to work. He has about given up, now, trying to find his two boys, William—or Bill, as he usually called him—and Charles, and what he wants is a home and some work by which he can make a living."

"Where is he going to work?" asked Nan.

"He is going to work in my lumberyard," answered her father. "I need a good, honest man, and though Hiram Hickson is a bit queer, I know he is good and honest. I am going to give him work."

"And where is he going to live?" asked Bert.

"Here, with us, for a while," answered Mr. Bobbsey. "We have room for him, and, as he is an old friend, and as he was once very kind to me, I want to do all I can for him.

"I said he could have a room in the house, but he says he is used to living alone of late, and so he is going to take one of the rooms over the stable, or what used to be the stable, before we got the automobile. Dinah and Sam have their rooms there, but there is another room for Mr. Hickson. So he will be like part of the family, and I want you children to be kind to him, as he has had trouble."

"I like him!" declared Bert.

"So do I," said Nan.

"Come, children," said their mother, "it is time to go to school; and there goes Mr. Hickson to work in daddy's lumberyard!"

CHAPTER V

NEWS FROM THE WEST

THE Bobbsey twins looked from the window and saw Hiram Hickson walking through the yard on his way from the garage. He had slept all night in the comfortable room in the former stable, where Dinah and Sam also lived.

As the old man passed he saw Flossie and Freddie and Bert and Nan looking from the window at him. He smiled up at the children, and waved his hand to them.

"He looks a little like Uncle Daniel, doesn't he?" remarked Bert.

"Yes," agreed Nan. "Only his hair is whiter. I guess he's had lots of troubles."

"Maybe about his two sons," Bert went on as the old man passed from sight toward the lumberyard. "I wish we could help him find them."

"I don't see how we could ever do that," returned Nan.

Flossie and Freddie stood with their noses pressed against the window glass, looking at Mr. Hickson until he was out of sight down the street. Then they got down off the chairs on which they had been kneeling, and Freddie asked:

"May I have an apple dumpling to take to school, Mother?"

"An apple dumpling to take to school!" she exclaimed. "Why, what in the world do you want to do that for?"

"I want it to eat at recess," explained the little fellow. "All the boys bring something to eat."

"And so do the girls," added Flossie. "I want something to eat, too. And Dinah is baking apple dumplings this morning—I smelled 'em when she opened the oven door."

"Well, I'm afraid apple dumplings are too big to take to school for a recess lunch," said Mrs. Bobbsey with a laugh. "I'll get Dinah to give you some cookies, though."

And Dinah not only gave some to Flossie

and Freddie, but to Bert and Nan. Then, happy and laughing, the Bobbsey twins started for school.

"Did you go down and see the big railroad wreck yesterday?" asked Danny Rugg of Bert at the school-yard gate.

"Sure I saw it," was the answer.

"And we got a man out of it, too," said Nan.

"You got a man out of the wreck! What do you mean?" exclaimed Danny. "Did you go down and pull him out?"

"No," Nan went on. "But we saw him, and he's at our house now."

"He works for my father," said Bert, and he told the story of Hiram Hickson, not speaking, however, about the two sons of the old man who had run away from him because of a quarrel. Bert did not think his father would like to have him tell this outside the family.

"I was right close to the engine when it puffed out a lot of steam," said Danny Rugg. "And I ran away like anything!"

"So did we!" said Bert.

All the boys and girls were talking about the wreck that morning, and because they had had such a curious part in it—having at their home one of the passengers who had been hurt—Bert and Nan were the center of a little throng that wanted to hear, over and over again, about it. So the older Bobbsey twins told all they knew concerning it from the time of having first heard about the wreck from Charley Mason until they came home accompanied by Hiram Hickson, who had been slightly hurt in the accident.

"Is he all right now?" Danny Rugg wanted to know.

"Oh, yes. He's gone to work in my father's lumberyard," explained Bert. "I'm going to stop in to see him this afternoon."

"Can't we go, too?" asked Danny, as he and Charley Mason walked back into the school with Bert, some of the talk having taken place at recess.

"Yes, I guess so," was the answer.

Bert often stopped at the lumberyard on his way home from school. He liked to play among the piles of logs and sawed boards, as did the other boys. Flossie and Freddie liked this, too, but they were not allowed to climb around on the lumber piles unless their father or some other older person was with them. Often Bert and Nan made "sea-saws" on a lumber pile, but to-day Nan wanted to hurry home with Grace Lavine and Nellie Parks, for they had a new story book they were reading together, and over which they were very much excited, each pretending she was one of the principal characters.

So, after school was out, and the cookies which Dinah had given the children had been eaten down to the last crumbs, Nan took Flossie and Freddie home with her, and Bert and some of his boy chums went to the lumberyard. On the way they made snowballs and threw them at trees and fences.

"There he is!" said Bert to Charley and Danny, as they saw Mr. Hickson measuring a pile of boards and marking the lengths down in a book. "There's the man that came out of the railroad wreck!"

"Pooh, he isn't hurt a bit!" exclaimed Danny Rugg. "I thought you said his head was cut, Bert Bobbsey!"

"'Tis cut!" declared Bert. "Isn't your head

cut, and weren't you hurt in the railroad wreck?" cried Bert, as Mr. Hickson waved his hand in greeting.

"Well, it isn't cut much—you can see where it is," and, taking off his hat, the old man showed the boys a piece of sticking plaster which had been put over the cut.

"There! What'd I tell you?" cried Bert.

Danny and Charley said nothing. They were satisfied now that they had actually seen the man himself and the cut he had got in the wreck.

The three boys played about on the lumber piles until it was time for them to go home, and Bert promised to bring his chums next day to have more fun on the masses of lumber. Some of the boards were so stacked up that there were spaces between, and these the boys played were "robber-caves."

It was nearing the end of winter when the railroad wreck had taken place. There was still plenty of snow and ice, but the sun was slowly working his way back from the south, where he had stayed so long, and each day brought spring nearer.

Mr. Hickson continued to live in his room over the Bobbsey garage. He liked it there, and he liked his work in the lumberyard. Mr. Bobbsey said the former Cedarville man was a good helper, and he was glad he had been able to hire him.

"And do you think he'll ever find his two boys?" asked Bert one day, when he and Nan had been talking to their father about Mr. Hickson.

"I'm afraid he'll never find them now, it has been so many years since they went away," explained Mr. Bobbsey. "They were boys then, sixteen or seventeen years old, and now they would be grown men. No, I don't believe Mr. Hickson will ever find his sons, though I wish he might, for I think it would make him much happier."

Bert and Nan wished they might help their father's friend to find his sons, but they did not see how it could be done. They even talked about it to Miss Pompret, the woman whose rare china they had so strangely discovered.

"Well, you Bobbsey twins are very lucky,"

said Miss Pompret, when Nan and Bert were at her house one early spring day. "You were very lucky about my china, and maybe you will be lucky about Mr. Hickson's sons. I hope he finds them. It is very sad to be old and to have no one in the world who really belongs to you. I hope you may be able to help him."

As has been said, the spring had come. The Bobbsey twins and the other children of Lakeport had made the most of winter while it lasted. They had built snow houses, snow men and had had snowball battles—at least—Bert, Charley Mason and Danny Rugg and the bigger boys, as well as Nan and her particular girl friends, had. The smaller ones, like Freddie, had coasted downhill on their sleds. This was fun in which Flossie also shared.

April came with plenty of showers, but the showers brought the May flowers, just as it says in the little verse. And then came June, which seemed the best month of all.

"Aren't you glad?" asked Bert of Nan, as the four Bobbsey twins were on their way to school one beautiful June morning, when the birds were singing and the flowers in the yards along the way were all in blossom.

"Glad? What for?" asked Nan.

"'Cause school will soon be over and we'll have a long vacation," answered Bert.

"Oh, that's so!" agreed Nan. "We have only a few more weeks of school. I hope I pass my examinations."

"I hope so, too," agreed Bert. "I'm going to study real hard."

"So'm I!" murmured Nan. "Oh, look! There goes Mr. Hickson on a pile of daddy's lumber!" she cried. "Maybe he'll give us a ride to school."

They shouted to the old man, who was now one of the best of Mr. Bobbsey's helpers in the lumberyard.

"Whoa, Esmeralda!" called Mr. Hickson to the horse he was driving. "What is it?" he asked of the Bobbsey twins, who were on the sidewalk. "Did you want me?" he asked. "The boards rattle so I couldn't hear what you said. There hasn't been another railroad wreck, has there?" and he smiled.

"No," answered Bert. "But could you give us a ride to school, if you're going down that way?"

"I am and I will," answered Mr. Hickson. "Wait a minute, Flossie and Freddie," he called to the smaller children. "I'll help you up. Now don't run away, Esmeralda!" he called to the horse.

"Oh, she won't run! She's the slowest horse daddy has!" laughed Nan.

"She's a good horse, though," said Mr. Hickson, as he carefully put Flossie and Freddie up on the boards on the wagon. "Yes, she's a good horse, but she's getting old—like me. Now are you up, Bert and Nan?" he asked, as he saw Bert helping his sister to her place.

"All ready!" Bert answered.

"Get along, Esmeralda!" called the man to the horse, and so the Bobbsey twins had a ride to school.

"Let's go down and play on your father's lumber piles to-day," said Danny Rugg to Bert, when school was out in the afternoon.

"Yes, we had a dandy time the other day!"

chimed in Charley Mason. "Let's go again."

"All right, we'll go!" agreed Bert.

But when he and the two boys reached the yard where the sweet-smelling boards were piled in great heaps, Bert saw his father coming from the office.

"May we play on the lumber?" asked Bert.

"Yes, but come home early," Mr. Bobbsey answered. "I'm going home now, Bert, and I think you'd better come soon."

"Is anything the matter?" asked the boy, for he knew it was early for his father to leave his office unless something had happened.

"Nothing serious," was the answer. "But I have just had some strange news from the West, and I want to tell your mother about it. The news came in a letter, and it may make a big change in our plans for the summer."

CHAPTER VI

AUNT EMELINE

WHEN Bert Bobbsey reached home that afternoon, having stopped his play on the lumber piles with Charley and Danny earlier than usual, the small boy saw his father and mother talking together on the side porch. Nan, Nellie Parks, and Grace Lavine were down in the yard under the shady grapevine playing.

"Well, I don't see anything for us to do except to go out West," Bert heard his father saying.

"Oh, do you really mean that?" cried the boy. "Are we going out West where there are Indians and cowboys and ponies and mountains and—and everything?"

His eyes were wide open with excitement.

"I didn't think you were around, or I wouldn't have spoken so loudly," said Mr. Bobbsey, with a laugh.

"But, tell me, Daddy! Are we really going out West?" asked Bert. "I've always wanted to go there, and I guess Nan has, too."

"Oh, you can depend upon it, Nan will always want to go where you go, and so will Flossie and Freddie, for that matter!" said Mrs. Bobbsey, with a laugh.

Bert had passed his small brother and sister as he entered the yard. They were playing with a little cart of Freddie's, and, as you can easily guess, Freddie was pretending he was a fireman.

"When are we going?" asked Bert. "Can't we go right away? School is almost over, and I know I'm going to pass 'cause the teacher said so. Nan is, too!"

"My, but you are getting in a hurry!" said Mr. Bobbsey. "We have only just begun to talk of the West and here you are stopping school to go."

"But what is it all about?" Bert went on. "Why do you have to go out West, Daddy? Aren't you going to have the lumberyard any more?"

"Oh, indeed I am, and perhaps a larger one

than before if things turn out the way I expect," answered Mr. Bobbsey. "But here comes Nan," he went on. "I think we might as well tell her and Bert all about it," he said to his wife. "If we go out West Bert and Nan will have to make believe they are almost grown up."

"What's it all about?" asked Nan, as she sat down on the steps beside her brother. Grace and Nellie had gone home to help their mothers get supper.

"Well, to begin at the beginning," said Mr. Bobbsey, "I had a letter to-day from some lawyers out West. Children, your mother has been left a cattle ranch and a lumber tract by a relative who died and made his will in your mother's favor."

"A cattle ranch?" cried Nan. "Oh, I know what that is! We have a picture of one in our geography! There's a lot of cattle in the picture, and cowboys are catching them with lassos."

"Yes, that's one of the things that happen on a ranch," said Mr. Bobbsey. "Well, your mother now owns one of those."

"She does?" cried Nan with wide-open eyes. "Oh, what are you going to do with it?"

"I'm going to be a cowboy on it!" decided Bert, as quickly as that. "I've always wanted to be a cowboy, and now I'm going to. When can I go on your ranch, Mother?" and jumping up eagerly he stood beside her, waiting for her answer.

"Oh, but, dear boy! I don't know anything about it yet," said Mrs. Bobbsey. "The letter has just come, and your father and I were talking over the news when you came. Poor Uncle Watson! I never knew him very well, though I had heard he was quite rich. But I never expected he would leave me his fine ranch, to say nothing of a lumber tract."

"What's a lumber tract?" Nan asked. "Is it a lumberyard like yours, Daddy?"

"No, my dear," answered Mr. Bobbsey. "A lumber tract is what you children would call big woods. It is a place where trees grow that may be cut down and made into lumber. All the boards and planks in my lumberyard were once big trees, growing out West, or up North, or down South. Now it seems that your mother's uncle owned a big forest of trees when lumber is cut, as well as owning a cattle ranch."

"And has he left them both to you?" asked Bert.

"Yes," his mother answered. "And the letter from the lawyers who made Uncle Watson's will tells me that I had better come out to look after the property that has been left to me."

"Are you going?" Nan wanted to know.

"I think I must," Mrs. Bobbsey replied. "It isn't every day I have so much property given me. I must go out West to look after it. But daddy is coming with me, so I'll be all right."

"Hurray!" cried Bert, tossing his hat into the air.

"What are you 'hurrahing' about?" asked his father.

"'Cause I'm going to be a cowboy on mother's ranch!" answered Bert. "Whoop-la! I'll be a lumberman, too, part of the time!"

"Now wait a minute, Son," said Mr. Bobbsey gently. "I don't want to spoil your fun, but we can't take you out West with us."

"You can't?" cried Bert. "Why. I though

we could all go—Nan, Flossie, Freddie, me everybody!"

"No, I don't see how we can take you children," said Mr. Bobbsey, while his wife also shook her head. "You see we have to leave in a hurry, and it would not do to take you youngsters out of school. We will not be gone longer than we can help."

"And have we got to stay here all alone?" asked Nan, and there was a suspicion of tears in her voice.

"You won't mind staying here," said her mother. "There will be Dinah to cook for you and to look after Freddie and Flossie. Sam will be around the house all the while, and there will be Mr. Hickson, too. Besides this we have a surprise for you."

"What is it?" cried Bert. "Are you going to take us after all? Oh, say you are! Tell me you were only fooling when you said we would have to stay here all alone!"

"No, I wasn't fooling," replied his mother. "I don't really see how we can take you children West with us. But the surprise is this. I am going to ask Aunt Emeline to come and stay with you, to keep house for you while your father and I are away. Aunt Emeline will come."

"Oh, Aunt Emeline!" gasped Nan.

"Aunt Emeline!" cried Bert. "Why she—she—"

Then he stopped short. He knew what he had been going to say was not polite.

"Aunt Emeline will be very kind to you," went on Mrs. Bobbsey. "I will go in and write to her now, asking her to come."

"And I must go in and telephone," said Mr. Bobbsey. "If I am to go West I shall have a lot of work to do to get ready."

Mr. and Mrs. Bobbsey entered the house, leaving Nan and Bert sitting out on the steps. For a moment or two the Bobbsey twins said nothing. They could hear Flossie and Freddie in the front yard laughing together as they played their games. Then Bert looked at Nan.

"Aunt Emeline!" he said, in a strange voice.

"Aunt Emeline!" responded Nan, and she sighed.

"I'll have to wipe my feet three times every

time I come into the house once!" went on Bert, in a grumbly voice. "She'll always be looking at my hands to see if they're clean and —and—Oh, I don't want Aunt Emeline to come!" he exclaimed.

"She never likes to have me run," said Nan, and her voice was gloomy. "She won't want me to have the other girls in here to play up in the attic, and she doesn't believe in eating cookies between meals!"

"It's going to be awful—terrible!" exclaimed Bert. "I know what I'm going to do!" he declared desperately.

"What?" asked Nan, in a frightened sort of voice.

"I'm going to run away, like Mr. Hickson's boys did!" Bert went on. "You can run away with me if you want to, Nan!" he added. "I'm going to be a cowboy and you can be the cook at the ranch."

"What ranch?" asked Nan.

"The one mother is going to get by Uncle Watson's will," explained her brother. "That's where I'm going to run to. I wouldn't run away to just any old place, but mother and father won't mind if I run off to our own ranch. They'll be glad to see me. Will you come, Nan?"

His sister shook her head.

"No," she answered. "Aunt Emeline is terrible, but she isn't bad enough to run away from, and maybe she'll be different now."

"She can't ever be any different," declared Bert. "I guess she means to be kind and good, but, say, a fellow can't be always washing his hands and wiping his feet!"

"And a girl's got to run and romp sometimes," added Nan. "But we'll have to do as father and mother want us to, I guess."

"Oh, I s'pose so!" agreed Bert. "Well, maybe I won't run away if you aren't coming with me. But I'd like to!" he said.

Flossie and Freddie heard something of the plans. They did not remember Aunt Emeline very well, though Bert and Nan easily recalled the queer old lady, who really was very particular when it came to children. She never had had any of her own, and perhaps this made a difference.

At first Flossie and Freddie had clamored to

be taken out West with their father and mother, as Bert and Nan had done. But when told they must stay at home and help Bert and Nan keep house, they seemed to be satisfied. They were some years younger than the older Bobbsey twins.

"I'll put out the fire if our house starts to burn while you're away," Freddie promised.

"There'll not be much danger of fire with Aunt Emeline here to look after things," said Mrs. Bobbsey. "I wouldn't leave my children with every one, but I know they'll be safe with Aunt Emeline," she said to Dinah.

"Yassum, dey's suah gwine to be *safe!*" declared the fat, jolly colored cook. "She suah will look after 'em! But will dey gets enough to *eat?* Dat's whut I'se askin' yo'!" and she looked earnestly at Mrs. Bobbsey.

"Well, you'll be doing the cooking as usual, Dinah," said the children's mother. "I depend on you to feed them well."

"Dat's all right, den!" exclaimed Dinah, with a satisfied air. "I knows she won't starve 'em at de table, even ef she suah has terrible 'tickler manners. But ef she says dey shan't eat 'tween meals, den I'll says to her as how dey can. I ain't gwine to hab mah honey lambs starvin', dat's whut I ain't!" and Dinah shook her woolly head.

"Oh, Aunt Emeline isn't as bad as all that," said Mrs. Bobbsey. "She is strict, I know, but it is for the children's good. I expect a letter from her very soon, saying when she can come. As soon as she can Mr. Bobbsey and I will start for the West."

Bert and Nan tried to be cheerful as the days passed, and they thought more and more of their father and mother going away from them. Flossie and Freddie had fretted a little at first, but, being younger, they were over it more quickly.

At last the letter came from Aunt Emeline. Bert and Nan were home when their mother read it to their father. A look of surprise came over Mrs. Bobbsey's face as she read.

"Dear me," she exclaimed, "this is quite surprising!"

"What is it?" asked her husband.

"Aunt Emeline can't come to stay with the children while we go West," was the answer.

"She says she is too old to take charge of a house and four children now, and she begs to be excused. Aunt Emeline isn't coming after all!"

Bert and Nan had hard work not to shout: Hurrah!

Mr. Bobbsey took the letter to read for himself.

"Then I'm sure I don't know what we're going to do," he said. "All our plans are made for going out West to look after the lumber tract and the cattle ranch. If Aunt Emeline can't come to stay with the children, what are we going to do?"

CHAPTER VII

HAPPY DAYS

MR. BOBBSEY sat looking at Aunt Emeline's letter, reading parts of it over again. Mrs. Bobbsey watched her husband. The Bobbsey twins looked at their father and mother. A great hope was beginning to come into the hearts of Bert and Nan.

As for Flossie and Freddie, they were rather too small to know what it was all about, but they realized that something had happened that did not happen every day.

"What's the matter, Mommie?" asked Freddie, slipping down out of his chair and going over to her. He saw that she was worried. "Have you got the toothache?" he wanted to know. Once Freddie's tooth had ached and he knew how it hurt.

"No, dear," answered Mrs. Bobbsey. "I haven't the toothache. But I have a letter from Aunt Emeline and she can't come to stay with you children while daddy and I go out West."

"Aunt Emeline not come?" repeated Freddie.

"No, dear. She thinks she is too old to look after you four lively youngsters. And perhaps she is right. I wouldn't want to make too much work for her."

"Aunt Emeline not coming!" said Freddie again in a thoughtful voice. "Ho! Then I go and get a cookie!"

Nan and Bert burst out laughing.

"What's the matter?" asked their father and mother, as Freddie slipped down out of his mother's lap, into which he had climbed, and started for the kitchen to find Dinah. "What made you laugh, Bert?" asked his mother.

"Oh, I guess Freddie must have heard Nan and me talking about Aunt Emeline not letting us have anything to eat except at meal time," replied Bert. "And, now she isn't coming, he thinks he can have a cookie whenever he wants it."

"Oh, I see!" and Mr. Bobbsey smiled.

"Well, Aunt Emeline may be strict, but she is a very good housekeeper. I am sorry she can not come to stay while we are in the West. I really don't know what we are going to do."

"Nor I," sighed Mrs. Bobbsey. "We counted on Aunt Emeline all the while, and now I don't know whom else I can get on such short notice. Can't we wait a while about going West?" she asked her husband.

"I don't very well see how we can wait," answered Mr. Bobbsey. "The tickets are bought, and all my plans are made. I have hired a man to come to the lumber office while I am away. I have written the men at the timber tract and at the cattle ranch that we are coming. Now, what are we to do?"

"We can't leave the children here alone," said Mrs. Bobbsey. "That is certain."

"No, we couldn't do that," agreed Mr. Bobbsey. "As good a cook as Dinah is, and careful as Sam is, we couldn't leave the children with them."

"Dinah gave me a cookie, an' she says she'll give you one, too, if you want it, Flossie," announced Freddie, coming into the room then, munching a sweet cake.

"Course I want it!" exclaimed the little "fat fairy," as her father called her, and she slipped out of her mother's lap, where she had climbed after Freddie got down, and, like her brother, hurried to the kitchen.

"Well, since we can't leave the children here at home by themselves, or only with Dinah and Sam," said Mr. Bobbsey, after a pause, "there is only one thing to do."

"You mean we must stay at home?" asked Mrs. Bobbsey, and the hearts of Bert and Nan felt very sad indeed.

"Stay at home? No, indeed!" exclaimed Mr. Bobbsey. "We must take the children with us!"

"Out West?" cried Mrs. Bobbsey.

"Yes, out West!" her husband said. "We'll take the children with us since Aunt Emeline can't come to stay with them."

"Hurray!" cried Bert.

"Oh, I'm so glad!" echoed Nan.

"Yes, that will be the best way out of it," went on Mr. Bobbsey to his wife, after Bert and Nan had stopped dancing around the room, hands joined, with Flossie and Freddie in the ring they made, the two younger twins each eating one of Dinah's cookies. "We'll take the Bobbsey twins out West."

"But what about school?" asked his wife, who just happened to think that the summer term would not end for about three weeks.

"Oh we don't need to go to school!" said Bert.

"We can take our books with us and study on the train," suggested Nan.

"I fear there wouldn't be much studying done," laughed Mrs. Bobbsey. "But do you really think we might take the children out of school?" she asked.

"That is something we will have to find out about," her husband answered. "Of course it will not be much loss to Flossie and Freddie, as they are not as far along in their studies as are Nan and Bert. But I wouldn't like to have them lose much of their lessons."

"Teacher said I was at the head of my class, and I'd pass easy!" declared Bert.

"And my teacher said I was one of her best

students," added Nan. She and Bert were in the same grade but in different classes.

"Well, since we really have to go out West to look after the lumber and cattle properties that are to be your mother's," said Mr. Bobbsey, "and since we must take you children with us, I'll see your teachers, Bert and Nan, and ask them if it will put you back much to lose the last two weeks of the term."

"Oh, goodie! Goodie!" shrieked Nan, jumping up and down.

"Hurray!" cried Bert. "Now I'm going to be a cowboy. Whoop!"

"Mercy me!" exclaimed their mother, covering her ears with her hands as Bert and Nan shouted loudly.

"Come on, Flossie!" called Freddie to his small sister. "Let's go and ask Dinah for more cookies."

That was Freddie's way of celebrating the good news.

Then came happy days.

Mr. Bobbsey, once he had made up his mind that the children were to go out West with him and his wife, went to the school and saw the teachers who had charge of Bert and Nan. He found that the older Bobbsey twins were so well along in their studies that it would not hold them back in the fall to stop now. So they were given permission to leave school before the regular time.

There was no trouble at all about Flossie and Freddie. They had simple lessons, and they could easily be taught at home to make up for the time they would lose.

It was arranged that Dinah and Sam should stay at home in the Bobbsey house to look after it during the summer, while Mr. and Mrs. Bobbsey and the twins went out West.

"And be sure to feed Snap!" said Bert to Sam, as the colored man was cutting the grass on the lawn one day, while the dog frisked about chasing sticks that Bert and Freddie tossed here and there for him.

"Oh, I won't forget Snap!" promised Sam.

"And you must give Snoop a saucer of milk every day, Dinah!" said Nan, as she rubbed the black cat which was purring around her legs.

"Oh, indeedy Snoop and I am mighty good

friends!" declared Dinah. "I suah won't forget to feed Snoop!"

Mr. Bobbsey bought other tickets, so he could take the children on the Western trip. He made all the arrangements, trunks were packed, and finally, one day, Bert and Nan and Flossie and Freddie said good-bye to their school chums.

"I'm going out West to learn to be a cowboy!" said Bert.

"I wish I was going!" exclaimed Danny Rugg.

"So do I," said Charley Mason.

"I'll see some Indians, too," Bert went on.

"And will you see those darling little pappooses they carry on their backs?" asked Nellie Parks.

"I guess I'll see them," Nan said. "I don't like Indian men and women, but the babies must be cute."

"Wouldn't it be great if you could get an Indian doll?" asked Grace.

"Indians don't have dolls!" declared Danny.

"Indian girls do!" exclaimed Nellie. "I saw a picture in one of my books of an Indian girl, and she had a doll made of corn silk and a corncob and some tree bark."

"What a funny doll!" exclaimed Grace. "Do try and bring one home, Nan!"

"I will," she promised.

Bert and Nan were so excited at the prospect of going West that if their father and mother had expected the children to pack the trunks and valises it never would have been done. But Mrs. Bobbsey knew better than to expect this. She and Dinah looked after the packing.

Flossie and Freddie, of course, were too small to do any of this, though one day Mrs. Bobbsey saw the little boy stuffing something into an old stocking.

"Freddie Bobbsey, what are you doing?" asked his mother.

"Dinah gave me some cookies," was the answer, "and I'm goin' to take 'em out West with me. Maybe I'll get hungry, an' maybe I'll get lost, or carried off by the Indians, an' then I'll have cookies to eat!"

"Oh, dear me! you can't take a lot of cookies in a stocking," laughed Mrs. Bobbsey.

"There'll be plenty to eat out West. As for getting lost, I suppose you will do that; you always have, but we manage to find you. However, I hope you won't get lost too often. And I don't think you'll be carried off by the Indians. Or, if so, they'd return you quickly."

The happy days seemed to grow happier as the time came nearer to take the train for the great West. One afternoon, the day before the Bobbsey twins were to start, Bert and Nan went down to their father's lumberyard office with a message sent by their mother.

"What's all this I hear about you?" asked Mr. Hickson, the old man who had been in the railroad wreck. He was out loading a wagon with boards. "What are you children going to do out West?" he asked them.

"I'm going to learn to be a cowboy," declared Bert.

"And I'm going to get an Indian doll!" said Nan.

"My goodness!" exclaimed the old man, smiling at the Bobbsey twins, for he liked them very much. "I hope you have a good time. That's what makes children happy—to have a good time. I wish I could find my children. I haven't seen my boys, Charley and Bill, for a long while. They must be grown-up men now. Yes, I certainly wish I could find Charley and Bill. It was all a mistake when they ran away from home. I wish I had them back," and slowly and sadly shaking his head he went on loading the lumber wagon.

Bert and Nan felt sorry for Mr. Hickson, and they wished they might help him find his "boys," as he called Bill and Charley, though, as he said, they must be grown men now. But Bert and Nan had too many things to think about in getting ready to go out West to feel sorry very long. They took the message to their father and then hurried home.

CHAPTER VIII

OFF FOR THE WEST

MONDAY morning was the day set for the start of the Bobbsey twins for the great West. They had said good-bye to their school friends the Friday before, and now, while the bells were ringing to call the other boys and girls to their classes, Bert, Nan, Flossie and Freddie stood on their front porch and watched their friends go past.

"Oh, but you are lucky!" called Danny Rugg to Bert, as the Bobbseys waved their hands to him.

"I wish I could be you!" added Charley Mason, as he swung his strap of books over his head. "I'm going out West to be a cowboy when I grow up."

"I'll tell you all about it when I come back," promised Bert.

Nan's girl friends, as they went past on their

way to school, blew kisses to her from their hands, and wished her all sorts of good luck.

Flossie and Freddie were too busy running around and playing hide-and-go-seek among the trunks to pay much attention to their little school friends who went past the house.

The trunks and valises had been stacked on the front porch, and in a little while Mr. Hickson was to come with his lumber wagon to take them to the station. Later the Bobbseys would go down in the automobile, one of the men from Mr. Bobbsey's office bringing it back. Sam Johnson, though he used to drive the Bobbsey horse when they had one, never could get used to an automobile, he said.

Snap, the jolly dog, seemed to know that something out of the ordinary was going on. He did not run about and play as he nearly always did, but stayed close to Bert and Nan. He seemed to know they were going away from him.

"You'll have to watch Snap," said Mrs. Bobbsey to Sam. "He may try to sneak after us and get on the train, as he did once before.

Mr. Bobbsey had to get off at the next station and bring him back."

"Yassum, I'll watch Snap," promised Sam. "But he suah does want to go wif yo' all pow'-ful bad!"

"I wish we could take Snap and Snoop!" said Bert.

"Oh, dear boy, we couldn't think of it!" exclaimed his mother. "We have a long way to travel to get to the West, and we couldn't look after a cat and a dog. They'll be much better off here at home."

"Snoop maybe will," agrued Bert, "'cause he doesn't like to have rough fun the way Snap does. But I guess my dog would like to see an Indian and some cowboys!"

However, the older Bobbsey twins knew it was out of the question to take their pets with them, so they made the best of it, Bert petting Snap and talking kindly to him. Snoop had gone out to the barn where he knew he might catch a mouse.

In a little while Mr. Hickson drove up for the trunks which were loaded on the lumber wagon.

"You're going to have a fine day to start for the West," said the old man, who had entirely got over his hurt got in the railroad wreck. "A very fine day!"

The June sun was shining, there was just enough wind to stir the leaves of the trees, and, as Mr. Hickson said, it was indeed a fine day for going out West, or anywhere else. Very happy were the Bobbsey twins.

With rattles and bangs, the trunks were piled on the lumber wagon, such valises as were not to be carried by Mr. or Mrs. Bobbsey, or Bert or Nan, were put in among the trunks. Flossie and Freddie were each to carry a basket which contained some things their mother thought might be needed on the trip.

"All aboard!" called Mr. Hickson, as he took his seat and gathered up the reins.

"That's what the conductor on the train says!" laughed Freddie, as he and Flossie had to stop playing hide-and-go-seek among the trunks.

"Well, I'm making believe this lumber wagon is a train," went on the old man. "I wish it was a train, and that I was going out West to find my two boys, Charley and Bill." Then he drove off with his head bowed.

"When do we start?" asked Bert. It was about the tenth time he had asked that same question that morning.

"We're going to leave soon now," his mother told him. "Don't go away, any of you. Nan, you look after Flossie and Freddie. It wouldn't surprise me in the least if Freddie were to get lost at the last minute."

Just then Freddie and his little sister were running around in the yard, playing tag, and neither of the smaller Bobbsey twins showed any signs of getting lost. But one never could tell what would happen to them—never!

Finally everything seemed to be in readiness for the start. The last words about looking after the house while the Bobbseys were in the West had been said to Sam and Dinah, and Mr. Bobbsey had telephoned his final message to his office to say that he was about to start. The automobile had been brought around, and Harry Truesdell, who was to drive it back from the station, was waiting.

"Come, children, we'll start now!" called

Mother Bobbsey. "Get the satchels you are to carry, Nan and Bert. Where are Flossie and Freddie?" she asked. "I want them to take their baskets."

"They were here a minute ago," replied Nan, looking around the yard for her smaller brother and Flossie.

"But they're not here now!" exclaimed Mrs. Bobbsey. "See if you can find them, Nan. Tell them we must leave now."

Nan set down the valise she had taken up and was about to go around to the back yard when some excited cries were heard. Dinah's voice sounded above the others.

"Heah, now, you stop dat, Freddie Bobbsey!" called the colored cook. "Whut are yo' doin'? Heah, Freddie, yo' let mah clothes line alone!"

There was a moment of silence, and then Dinah's voice went on.

"Oh, land o' massy! Oh, I 'clare to goodness, yo' suah has gone an' done it now! Oh, mah po' li'l honey lamb! Oh, Freddie, look what you has gone an' done!"

At this moment the crying voice of Flossie

dat so much!" she said, as she wiped away the tears from the face of the frightened Flossie. "I kin wash de sheets ober ag'in. But I'm so s'prised dat Freddie done scared his li'l sister, dat's whut I am. Freddie done scared honey lamb mos' to pieces!"

"I—I didn't mean to," repeated Freddie.

"But did you really cut down Dinah's wash line?" his mother asked him, when it had been found that Flossie was only frightened and not hurt.

"I—I cut off a little piece," said Freddie, showing a dangling end in his hand. "I didn't think it would fall down. I didn't mean to make it."

"But what made you cut any of it?" asked his father, tying the cut ends together while Dinah took up the sheets which had fallen to the ground and had some black spots on them. "Why did you cut the clothes line, Freddie?"

Mr. Bobbsey did not call his little boy "fireman" now. That was a pet name, and used only when Freddie had been good, and he had been a little bad now, though perhaps he did not mean to.

"I—I cut the line to get a piece of rope," said Freddie.

"What did you want a piece of rope for?" asked his father.

"I wanted to make a lasso to lasso Indians as Bert's going to do," Freddie answered. "I wanted a piece of clothes line for a lasso. But I didn't mean to make the clothes come down."

"No, I don't guess you did," said Dinah, as she came out of the laundry with the sheets which she had rinsed clean. "Ole Dinah done gwine to forgib her honey lamb 'cause he's gwine away far off from her. An' Dinah's other honey lamb didn't get hurted any. It was only two sheets an' Dinah's done washed 'em clean again. But don't you go lassoin' any Injuns, Freddie! Dey mightn't like it."

"No, I won't!" promised the little fellow.

"And don't cut any more clothes lines," added his father.

"No, sir, I won't!"

Freddie was ready to promise anything, now that he found nothing serious had happened. At first, after he had cut the rope and let the sheets down on Flossie's head as she was running through the yard, Freddie had been very much frightened.

"Well, I'm glad it was no worse," said Mrs. Bobbsey, as she straightened Flossie's hat, which had been knocked to one side. "Now we must hurry, or we'll be late for the train."

"Yes, come along!" called Mr. Bobbsey.

Freddie gave up the bread knife to Dinah, the last good-byes were said, and the children started for the automobile. Snap leaped around Bert, barking and whining.

"Better tie up the dog, Sam, or he'll follow us," said Mr. Bobbsey.

"Yes, sah. I'll do dat."

Poor Snap was led away whining. He did not want to be left behind, but it had to be.

"Good-bye!" called Bert to his pet. "Good-bye, Snap!"

Flossie took up her basket, and Freddie had his. Each one had something to carry. Into the automobile they hurried and soon they were on the way to the station to take the train for the West.

They did not have many minutes to wait. Harry Truesdell sat in the automobile until

Mr. Bobbsey and the family should be aboard the train before he went back to the garage.

The Bobbsey twins were standing on the station platform. Mr. Bobbsey was talking to a man he knew, and Mrs. Bobbsey was speaking to two friends. Bert and Nan were putting pennies in a weighing machine to see how heavy they had grown, and Freddie was looking at the pictures on the magazine covers at the news stand.

Suddenly Flossie, who had set her basket down on one of the outside seats, gave a cry.

"What's the matter?" asked her mother, turning quickly. "What is it, Flossie?"

"Oh, my basket! My basket!" cried the little girl. "There's something in it! Something alive! Look, it's wriggling!"

And, surely enough, the basket she had carried, was "wriggling." It was swaying from side to side on the station seat.

CHAPTER IX

DINNER FOR TWO

FREDDIE BOBBSEY, called away from looking at the magazine pictures on the news stand, came running over when he heard Flossie shout.

"What's the matter?" asked the little boy. "Did something else fall on you, Flossie, like the sheets flopping over your head?"

"No, nothing falled on me!" exclaimed Flossie. "But look! Look at my basket! It's wriggling!"

"There's something in it!" exclaimed Mrs. Bobbsey, while her husband quickly hurried away from the man to whom he was talking, and prepared to see what the matter was. "There's something in your basket, Flossie! Did you put anything in?"

"No, Mother!" answered the little girl. "I just put in the things you gave me. And just before I came away I took off the cover to put in some cookies Dinah handed me."

"I think I can guess what happened," said Mr. Bobbsey. "While the cover was off the basket something jumped in, Flossie."

"Oh, I see what it is! A little black squirrel!" cried Nan.

"Squirrels aren't black!" Bert said. There were some squirrels in the trees near the Bobbsey house, but all Bert had ever seen were gray or reddish brown.

"It's something furry, anyhow," Nan went on. "I can see it through the cracks in the basket."

And just then, to the surprise of every one looking on, including the Bobbsey twins, of course, the cover of the basket was raised by whatever was wriggling inside, and something larger than a squirrel, but black and furry, looked out.

"Gee!" exclaimed Bert.

"Oh, it's Snoop!" cried Nan.

"It's our cat!" added Freddie.

"In my basket!" exclaimed Flossie. "How did you get there, Snoop?" she asked, as Bert took the cat up in his arms, while the other passengers at the station laughed.

"Perhaps Snoop felt lonesome when he knew you were going to leave him," said Mrs. Bobbsey. "And when you took off the cover of your basket, Flossie, to put in the cookies Dinah gave you, Snoop must have seen his chance and crawled in."

"He kept still all the way in the auto, so we wouldn't know he was there," added Nan.

"Maybe he thought we'd take him with us," said Bert. "Did you, Snoop?" he asked. But the big black cat, who must have found it rather hard work to curl up in the basket, snuggled close to Bert, who was always kind to animals.

Just then the whistle of the train was heard down the track.

"Dear me! what shall we do?" cried Mrs. Bobbsey. "We can't possibly take Snoop with us, and we can't leave him here at the depot."

"Harry will take Snoop back home in the auto," said Mr. Bobbsey.

"Yes, give him to be—I'll be careful of him,"

promised the young man from the lumberyard office, and Bert carried his pet over to the waiting automobile.

Snoop mewed a little as Bert put the big black cat into Harry's arms.

"Good-bye, Snoop!" Bert said, patting his pet on the head.

"Come, Bert, hurry!" called his father.

Then, as the train pulled into the station, Bert ran back and caught up his valise. The other Bobbsey twins took up their things, Flossie put back on her basket the cover the cat had knocked off in getting out, and soon they were all on the train.

"All aboard!" called the conductor, and, as the engine whistled and the cars began to move, Bert and Nan looked from the windows of their seats and had a last glimpse of Snoop being held in Harry's arms, as he sat in the automobile.

Flossie and Freddie forgot all about their cat, dog, and nearly everything in Lakeport in their joy at going out West. For they were really started on their way now, after several little upsets and troubles, such as the clothes line coming down on Flossie, and the cat hiding himself away in the basket.

"Well, now I can sit back and rest," said Mrs. Bobbsey, with a sigh of relief. "I know the children are all here, and they can't get lost for a while, at least, and I don't see what mischief they can get into here."

Now, indeed, the children were all right for a time. Freddie sat with his father, next to the window, and Flossie was in the seat with her mother pressing her little nose close against the glass, so she would not miss seeing anything, as the train flew along.

Bert and Nan were sitting together, Nan being next to the window. Bert had, very politely, let his sister have that place, though he wanted it himself. However, before the first part of the journey was over there was a seat vacant on the other side of the car, and Bert took that. Then he, too, had a window.

Bert and Nan noticed, as the train passed Mr. Bobbsey's lumberyard, Mr. Hickson standing amid a pile of boards. The old man did not see the children, of course, for the train was going rather swiftly, but they saw him.

"I wish we could help him find his two sons," said Nan to Bert.

"Yes, I wish we could," Bert answered "But it's so long ago maybe Mr. Hickson wouldn't know his boys even if he saw them again."

"He'd know their names, wouldn't he?" Nan asked.

"Yes, I s'pose he would," Bert replied.

Then the older Bobbsey twins forgot about Mr. Hickson in the joys and novelty of traveling.

The Bobbseys were going to travel in this train only as far as a junction station. There they would change to a through train for Chicago, and in that big western city they would again make a change. On this through train Mr. Bobbsey had had reserved for him a drawing room. That is part of the sleeping car built off from the rest at one end.

On arriving at the junction the Bobbseys left the train they had been on since leaving Lakeport and got on the through train, which drew into the junction almost as soon as they did. They went into the little room at the end of the sleeping coach which Mr. Bobbsey had had reserved for them. In there the twins had plenty of room to look from the windows, as no other passengers were in with them.

"It's just like being in our own big automobile," said Nan, and so it was. The children liked it very much.

The trip to Chicago would take a day and a night, and Flossie and Freddie, as well as Bert and Nan, were interested in going to sleep on a train in the queer little beds the porter makes up from what are seats in the daytime.

It was not the first time the children had traveled in a sleeping car, but they were always interested. It did seem queer to them to be traveling along in their sleep.

"Almost like a dream," Nan said, and I think she was quite right.

"Where's my basket?" Flossie asked, after they had ridden on for about an hour.

"Do you want to see if Snap is in it this time?" her father jokingly inquired.

"Snap's too big to get in my basket," Flossie answered. "He's a big dog. But I want to get some of the cookies Dinah gave me. I'm hungry."

"So'm I!" cried Freddie, who had been looking from the window. "I want a cookie too!"

"Dinah gave me some for you," Flossie said, and, when her basket had been handed down from the brass rack over the seat, she searched around in it until she had found what she was looking for—a bag of molasses and sugar cookies.

"Oh, Dinah does make such good cookies!" said Flossie, with her mouth half full, though, really, to be polite, I suppose, she should not have talked that way.

"Shall we get any cookies out on the cattle ranch?" asked Nan. "If we don't, Flossie and Freddie will miss them."

"Oh, they have cooks on ranches, same as they do in lumber camps," Bert declared. "I saw a picture once of a Chinese cook on a cattle ranch."

"Can a Chinaman cook?" asked Nan, in surprise. "I thought they could only iron shirts and collars."

"Some Chinese are very good cooks," explained Mr. Bobbsey. "And Bert is right when he says that on some ranches in the West a Chinese man does the cooking. I don't know whether we shall find one where we are going or not."

"Are we going to the lumber tract first, or to the ranch?" asked Bert.

"To where the big trees grow," answered his father. "The tract your mother is going to own is near a place called Lumberville. It is several hundred miles north and west of Chicago. We will stop off there, and go on later to the ranch. That is near a place called Cowdon."

"What funny names," laughed Bert. "Lumberville and Cowdon. You would think they were named after the trees and the cows."

"I think they were," his father said. "Out West they take names that mean something, and Lumberville and Cowdon just describe the places they are named after."

While Flossie and Freddie were looking from the window of the coach in which they were riding, while Bert and Nan were telling one another what good times they would have on the ranch and in the lumber camp, and while Mr. and Mrs. Bobbsey were discussing matters about the trip, there came a knock on the door.

Mr. Bobbsey opened it and a lady came in, saying:

"I am so glad to see you! I am traveling to Chicago all alone, and I saw you get on as I looked from my window in the next car. I came back to speak to you."

"Why, it's Mrs. Powendon!" exclaimed Mrs. Bobbsey as she saw a lady whom she had first met at a Red Cross meeting. Mrs. Powendon lived in a village near Lakeport, and often came over to see Mr. and Mrs. Bobbsey and other friends. "I am very glad you saw us and came in to see us," went on Mrs. Bobbsey. "Do sit down! So you are going to Chicago?"

"Yes. But what takes you away from Lakeport?"

"I don't suppose you heard the news, but an old uncle of mine, whom I had not seen for years, died and left me a western lumber tract and a cattle ranch. Mr. Bobbsey and I are on our way there now to look after matters, and we had to take the children with us."

"And I suppose they were very sorry about that," said Mrs. Powendon with a smile, as she looked at Nan and Bert.

"Oh, no!" exclaimed Bert. "Indeed we weren't sorry! We're going to have fine times!"

Then Mrs. Powendon sat down and began talking to Mr. and Mrs. Bobbsey, while Nan and Bert looked at magazines their father had bought for them from the train boy.

No one paid much attention to Flossie and Freddie, and it was not until some little time later that Mrs. Bobbsey, looking around the drawing room, exclaimed:

"Where are they?"

"Who?" asked her husband.

"Flossie and Freddie. They aren't here!"

That was very evident. There was no place in the little room for them to hide, and yet the children could not be seen.

"Oh!" exclaimed Mrs. Bobbsey, "can they have fallen off the train?"

"Of course not!" answered her husband.

"They must just have gone outside in the car. I'll look."

Mr. Bobbsey was about to open the door when a knock came on it, and, as the door swung back, the face of a colored porter looked in. The man wore a white jacket.

"'Scuse me, sah," he said, talking just as Sam Johnson did, "but did you-all only want dinnah for two?"

"Dinner for two? What do you mean?" asked Mr. Bobbsey.

"Why, dey's two li'l children in de dinin' car. Dey says as how dey belongs back yeah, an' dey's done gone an' ordered dinnah for two—jest fo' der own selves—jest two! I was wonderin' ef you-all folks wasn't goin' to eat!"

CHAPTER X

FREDDIE, AS USUAL

"DINNER for two! Little children!" exclaimed Mr. Bobbsey.

"It is Flossie and Freddie!" cried his wife. "Where is the dining car?"

The waiter from the dining car, who had come back to the sleeping car where the Bobbseys had their places, smiled as he finished telling about the two children.

"Dey's right up forward in my dinin' car," he said to Mrs. Bobbsey. "An' dey is all right, too, lady! I tooked good keer ob 'em. Dey jest walked right in, laik dey owned de place, an' I says to 'em, what will dey hab?

"Dey tells me dat dey done want dinnah fo' two, an' I starts to gib it to 'em, but de conductor says as how dey belonged to a party back heah, an' mebby de odder folks would want somethin' to eat, too. An', as anyhow, dey had bettah be tol'."

"I'm hungry!" exclaimed Bert.

"So'm I!" added Nan.

"Dear me!" exclaimed Mrs. Bobbsey. "I must go and see about them."

"We will all go," said Mr. Bobbsey. "I did not know it was so near lunch time. But I suppose Freddie and Flossie never forget anything so important as that."

"Trust children to remember their meals!" said Mrs. Powendon. "I fear I am to blame for your two little ones running away."

"Oh, no," murmured Mr. Bobbsey.

"How?" asked Mrs. Bobbsey.

"By coming in here, and talking to you. Probably I left the door of your drawing room open. Flossie and Freddie must have slipped out that way."

"Very likely they did," said their father. "But no great harm is done. We will all go to lunch now. Won't you come with us, Mrs. Powendon?"

"Thank you, I will," answered the lady who had come visiting, and so the rest of the

Bobbseys and their friend went to the dining car.

There, surely enough, seated at a little table all by themselves, were Flossie and Freddie. The two tots looked up as their father and mother, with Nan and Bert and Mrs. Powendon, came into the car.

"I'm going to have a piece of pie!" shouted Freddie so loudly that every one in the car must have heard, for nearly every one laughed.

"So am I going to have pie!" echoed Flossie, and there was another laugh.

"Well, what have you children to say for yourselves?" asked Mrs. Bobbsey, in the voice she used when she was going to scold just a little bit. "What have you to say, Freddie?"

"I like it in here!" he said. "It's a nice place to eat."

"And I like it, too!" added Flossie.

Mr. and Mrs. Bobbsey tried not to laugh. "But you shouldn't have slipped away while we were talking and come in here all alone," went on Mother Bobbsey. "Why did you do it?"

"I was hungry," said Freddie, and that seemed to be all there was to it.

"Our cookies were all in crumbs," explained Flossie. "They wasn't a one left in my basket. I was hungry, too."

'I presume that's as good an excuse as any," said Mr. Bobbsey, with a laugh. "And so we'll all sit down and have lunch."

And while they were eating Flossie and Freddie told how they had slipped out, when their mother and father were busy talking to Mrs. Powendon, and while Bert and Nan were looking out of the window. They had been in dining cars on railroad trains before, and so they knew pretty nearly what to do.

But when they ordered dinner for themselves, or at least told the smiling, black waiter to bring them something to eat, the Pullman conductor, who had seen the children in the sleeping coach, suspected that all was not right, so he sent the waiter back to tell Mrs. Bobbsey about Flossie and Freddie.

"And you mustn't do it again," said Mrs. Bobbsey, when the story had been told.

"No'm, we won't!" promised Freddie.

"No, he won't do just this again," said Bert with a laugh to Nan. "But he'll do something else just as queer."

And of course Freddie did.

After lunch Mrs. Powendon went back to her car, and the Bobbseys took their seats in the drawing room which they occupied. The meal and the riding made Flossie and Freddie sleepy, so their mother fixed a little bed for them on the long seat, and soon they were dreaming away, perhaps of cowboys and Indians and big trees being cut down in the forest to make lumber for playhouses.

The train rumbled on, stopping now and then at different stations, and, after a while, even Bert and Nan began to get tired of it, though they liked traveling.

"How much farther do we have to go?" asked Bert, as the afternoon sun began to go down in the west.

"Oh, quite a long way," his father answered. "We are not even in Chicago yet. We shall get there to-morrow morning, and stay there two days. Then we will go on to Lumberville. How long we shall stay there I do not know. But as soon as we can attend to the business and get matters in shape, we will go on to Cowdon."

"That's the place I want to get to!" exclaimed Bert. "I want to see some Indians and cowboys."

"There may not be any there," said his mother.

"What! No cowboys on a ranch?" cried the boy.

"Why, Mother!" exclaimed Nan.

"I meant Indians," said Mrs. Bobbsey. "Of course there'll be cowboys to look after the cattle, but Indians are not as plentiful as they once were, even out West."

"I only want to see an Indian baby and get an Indian doll," put in Nan. "I don't like grown-up Indians. They have a lot of feathers on, like turkeys."

"That's what I like!" Bert declared. "If I wasn't going to be a cowboy I'd be an Indian, I guess."

Night came, and when the electric lights in the cars were turned on Freddie and Flossie awakened from their nap.

"How do you feel?" asked his mother, as she smoothed her little boy's rumpled hair.

"I—I guess I feel hungry!" he said, though he was still not quite awake.

"So'm I!" added Flossie. You could, nearly always, depend on her to say and do about the same things Freddie did and said.

"Well, this is a good time to be hungry," said Mr. Bobbsey with a laugh. "I just heard them say that dinner was being served in the dining car. We'll go up and eat again."

After dinner the porter made up the funny little beds, or "berths," as they are called, and soon the Bobbsey twins had crawled into them and were asleep.

It must have been about the middle of the night that Mrs. Bobbsey, who was sleeping with Flossie on one side of the aisle, heard a noise just outside her berth. It was as if something had fallen to the floor with a thud. She opened the curtains and looked out. Freddie and his father had gone to sleep in the berth just across from her, but now she saw a little white bundle lying on the carpeted floor of the car.

"What is that? Who is it?" the mother of the twins exclaimed.

Mr. Bobbsey poked his head out from between his curtains.

"What's the matter?" he asked. "Anything gone wrong?" he added sleepily.

"Look!" exclaimed his wife. "What's that?" and she pointed to the bundle lying on the floor.

"That? Oh, that must be *Freddie,*" answered Mr. Bobbsey. "As usual he's done something we didn't expect. He's fallen out of his car bed."

CHAPTER XI

IN CHICAGO

SURELY enough Freddie Bobbsey had fallen out of bed, or his "berth," as beds are called in sleeping cars. The little fellow had been resting with his father, and on the inside, too. But he must have become restless in his sleep, and have crawled over Mr. Bobbsey.

At any rate, when Freddie fell out he made a thud that his mother, in her berth across the aisle, had heard.

But the carpet on the floor of the car was so soft, and Freddie was such a fat, chubby little fellow, and he was so sound asleep, that he was not at all hurt in his tumble, and he never even awakened. He just went on sleeping, right there on the floor.

"Yes," said Mr. Bobbsey with a smile at his wife as he picked Freddie up, "you can generally depend on his doing something unusual, or different. Well, he's a nice little boy," he murmured softly, as he picked up the "fireman" and put him back in the berth.

Even then Freddie did not completely wake up. But he murmured something in his dreams, though Mr. Bobbsey heard only a few words about Indians and cowboys and sugar cookies.

"He's hungry even in his sleep!" said the father, with a silent laugh.

The other Bobbsey twins knew nothing of what had happened until morning, when they were told of Freddie's little accident.

"And did I really fall out of bed?" asked Freddie, himself as much surprised as any one.

"You certainly did!" laughed his mother. "At first I was startled, being aroused so suddenly, but I saw that you were still sleeping and I knew you couldn't be hurt very much."

"I didn't even feel it!" laughed Freddie. "And now I want my breakfast!"

"Dear me! You want to eat again, after dreaming about sugar cookies?" cried Mr. Bobbsey, and he told his little boy what he had heard him say in his sleep. "Well, we had all better go to the dining car again. It will be our last meal there."

"Our last meal!" cried Bert. "Aren't we going to eat again?"

"Not on this train," his father answered. "We'll be in Chicago in time for dinner."

Breakfast over, the Bobbseys began gathering up their different things to be ready to get out at Chicago when the train should reach that big and busy city.

It was about ten o'clock when the station was reached, and the Bobbsey twins thought they had never been in such a noisy place, nor one in which there were more people.

But Daddy Bobbsey had traveled to Chicago before, and he knew just what to do and where to go. He called an automobile, and in that the whole family rode to the hotel where they were to stay while they were in the city.

Two days were to be spent in Chicago, which Mrs. Bobbsey had not visited for some time. She wanted to look around a little, and show the children the various sights. Mr. Bobbsey planned to attend to some business in the "Windy City," as Chicago is sometimes called.

Both Mr. and Mrs. Bobbsey wanted their children to see all there was to be seen.

"Travel will broaden their minds," Mrs. Bobbsey had said to her husband when they had talked the matter over one night after the twins had gone to bed. "Just see how much they learned when we took them to Washington."

"They not only learned something, but they brought back something—I mean Miss Pompret's china pieces," said Mr. Bobbsey. "Yes, traveling is good for children if they do not do too much of it."

So when the Bobbsey twins reached the big Chicago hotel they were not as strange and surprised as they would have been if they had never been at a hotel before.

"I like this better than the hotel we stayed at in Washington," said Nan to Bert, as they were shown to their rooms, after riding up in an elevator.

"Yes, you can see lots farther," agreed Bert, as he glanced from one of the windows.

"I didn't mean that," his sister said. "I mean the curtains and chairs and such things are ever so much nicer."

"You can't eat curtains!" exclaimed Bert. "And I'm hungry. I hope they have good things to eat."

"I think they will," his father remarked, with a laugh.

And when, a little later, they went down to the dining room, the Bobbsey twins found that it was a very good hotel, indeed, as far as things to eat were concerned.

Though Mrs. Bobbsey was very much interested in Chicago, and though Mr. Bobbsey was glad to get there to look after some matters of his lumber business, I must admit that none of the Bobbsey twins thought a great deal of the big city.

"'Tisn't any different from New York!" declared Bert, as he looked at the big buildings, the elevated roads, the street cars and the hurrying crowds. "I wouldn't know but what I was in New York."

"Yes, in some ways it is much like New York," his mother agreed.

"But there isn't any big lake in New York, such as there is here," said Nan.

"Well, I guess the New York Atlantic Ocean is bigger than Lake Michigan," returned Bert. "And the ocean has salt water in it, too, and Lake Michigan is fresh!"

"That makes it better!" declared Nan, who decided then and there to "stick up" for Chicago. "If you're thirsty you can't drink the salty ocean water, but you could drink the lake water."

"Well, maybe that's better," admitted Bert. "I didn't think of that."

And when he and the other children had been taken by their father out to the city lake front, and had seen the bathing beach, Bert had to admit that, after all, Chicago was just as good as New York. But he would not say it was better.

As for Flossie and Freddie, any place was nice to them if they had Bert and Nan and daddy and mother along. The smaller twins seemed to have fun over everything; even riding up and down in the hotel elevator amused them.

After a day of sight-seeing about Chicago, Mrs. Bobbsey was rather tired, and she thought the children were, too, for she told them they had better go to bed early, as they would still have another day to-morrow to see things.

"Oh, I don't want to go to bed!" exclaimed Bert. "There's a nice moving picture in the theater near this hotel! It's all about Indians and cowboys, and daddy said he'd take us after supper. Anyhow, he said he'd take Nan and me."

"If he said so I suppose he will," said Mrs. Bobbsey. "But I can't let Flossie and Freddie go, and I am too tired to go myself."

"Oh, I want to see the Indians!" cried Freddie when he heard what was being talked about.

"No, dear. You and Flossie stay here with me in the hotel, and I'll read you a story," promised his mother. She knew by his tired little legs and his sleepy eyes that she would not have to read more than one story before he and Flossie would be fast asleep.

And so it proved. Mr. Bobbsey took Nan

and Bert to the moving picture theater a few doors from the hotel, promising to bring them back early, so they would not loose too much sleep. Then Mrs. Bobbsey sat down to read to Flossie and Freddie.

Just as she had expected, before she reached the end of the story two little heads were nodding and four sleepy eyes could hardly keep open.

"Bed is the place for my tots!" said Mrs. Bobbsey softly, and soon Flossie and Freddie were slumbering together.

Mr. Bobbsey came in with Nan and Bert about an hour later, the pictures having been enjoyed very much.

"I surely am going to be a cowboy!" declared Bert. "I can easily be one on the ranch you are going to own, can't I, Mother?"

"We'll see," replied Mrs. Bobbsey, with a quiet smile at her husband.

Then Nan and Bert went to bed and were soon asleep.

"Well, I hope Freddie doesn't fall out of bed again to-night, and wake me up," said the children's mother.

"So do I," echoed her husband. "I think we shall all rest well to-night."

But trying to sleep in a big city hotel is quite different from trying to sleep in one's own, quiet home. There seemed to be even more noises than on the railroad train, where the motion of the cars, and the clickety-click of the wheels, appears to sing a sort of slumber song. So it was that in the Chicago hotel Mrs. Bobbsey did not get to sleep as soon as she wished.

However, after a while, she did close her eyes, and then she knew nothing of what happened until she heard a loud whistle, something like that of a steam locomotive outside. She also heard some shouting, and then she felt some one shaking her and a voice saying:

"Mother! Mother! Come and see 'em!"

Quickly Mrs. Bobbsey opened her eyes, and, in the dim light that came from the hall, she saw Freddie standing beside her bed.

"What is it?" she asked, sitting up and taking her little boy by the arm.

"They're here! Come and see 'em!" exclaimed Freddie again. "I heard 'em, and I saw 'em! There's a whole lot of 'em!"

"What in the world is the child talking about?" said Mrs. Bobbsey, and then her husband awakened.

"What's the matter now?" he asked sleepily. "Oh, is that you, Freddie?" he went on, as he saw the little Bobbsey twin. "What's the matter? Did you fall out of bed again?"

"No, Daddy. But there's a whole lot of fire engines down in the street. I saw 'em!"

"Fire engines!" cried Mrs. Bobbsey. "Oh, Dick! do you suppose—"

What Mrs. Bobbsey feared was that the hotel was on fire, but she did not want to say this in Freddie's hearing.

"There's a great big engine, and it's puffing and blowing out sparks," said the little fellow.

"Freddie ought to know a fire engine by this time when he sees one," Mr. Bobbsey said. "I'll get up and have a look. There may be a small fire next door. Don't get frighttened."

Mrs. Bobbsey got up too and slipped on a bath robe, then, taking Freddie by the hand she went with him to the window in his room where he had said he had looked out and had seen the fire engine.

But as Mr. Bobbsey took a look he laughed and said:

"This is the time you were fooled, little fireman! That isn't a fire engine at all. That's some sort of engine they use for fixing the streets. They have to work on the streets here after dark, as there are too many automobiles and wagons on them in the day time There isn't any fire, Freddie!"

"Maybe there'll be a fire to-morrow," returned Freddie, rather hopefully, though of course he did not really want any one's house to be burned.

"Well, there isn't a fire to-night—at least not around here," said Mr. Bobbsey. "Now we can go back to bed."

Bert nor Nan nor Flossie had been awakened by the noise which roused Freddie. And really it had sounded like a fire engine. A gang of men with a big steam roller was at work in the street just below the little Bobbsey twins' window. And smoke and sparks were spouting from the boiler of the steam roller just as they often spouted from a fire engine.

Freddie slept soundly after that little excitement, and the Bobbsey family did not get up very early the next morning, as they were all tired from their travel.

"Do we go on to Lumberville to-day, Daddy?" asked Bert after breakfast in the hotel.

"Yes, we start this evening and travel all night again," his father answered. "In the morning, or rather, about noon to-morrow, we ought to be at the lumber tract."

"And shall I see 'em cut down trees?" asked Freddie.

"They don't do much cutting down of trees in the summer," said Mr. Bobbsey. "Winter is the time for that. Still there may be some cutting going on, and I hope you can see it."

"I'd rather see cowboys," put in Bert. "That was a dandy picture of cowboys lassoing wild steers last night."

"I wish I could go and see that!" exclaimed Freddie.

"Some other time, maybe," his mother

promised. "I am going to take you all shopping now, and buy you each something."

Nan's eyes shone in delight at this, for she liked, very much, to go shopping with her mother.

Mr. Bobbsey still had some business to look after, and when he had left the hotel, promising to come back at lunch time, Mrs. Bobbsey gathered her four "chickens" as she sometimes called them, about her, and made ready to go shopping. No, I am wrong. She only gathered three "chickens." Freddie was missing.

"Where can he be?" asked his mother. "He was right by that window a moment ago!"

"Oh, I hope he hasn't fallen out!" shrieked Nan.

CHAPTER XI

NEARING LUMBERVILLE

BERT BOBBSEY was the first to spring to the window and look down when his sister said this. As the rooms Mr. Bobbsey had taken were on the tenth floor it would have been quite a fall for Freddie if he had tumbled out. But after one look Bert said:

"Freddie couldn't have fallen from here. There's an iron railing all around the outside of the window, and even Freddie couldn't get through."

"I wonder where he is!" exclaimed Mrs. Bobbsey. "I'm sure I saw him here a moment ago!"

"Yes, he was here," said Nan. "I washed a speck of dirt off his chin, and then Flossie wanted me to wash her hands."

"But I washed my own hands, I did!" exclaimed Flossie, looking at her pink palms.

"And the soap slid all over the floor and every time I picked it up it slid some more; didn't it, Nan?" she asked with a laugh.

"Yes," answered the older girl. "But where can Freddie be?"

"That's what I'm wondering," added Mrs. Bobbsey. "We must find him."

"I guess he went out into the hall," said Bert. "There's a boy in the rooms next door about as old as Freddie, and I saw them talking together yesterday."

Mrs. Bobbsey hurried into the hall outside their apartment in the hotel. Bert, Nan and Flossie followed, Flossie still laughing at the funny way the cake of soap had slid around the bathroom when she washed her hands.

Mrs. Bobbsey looked up and down the corridor, but she saw nothing of her little boy. She was hurrying toward the elevators, where the red light burned at night, when she met one of the chambermaids who looked after the rooms and made up the beds.

"Are you looking for your little boy?" asked the maid, smiling pleasantly at Mrs. Bobbsey and the children.

"Yes, I am," answered Freddie's mother. "Have you seen him?"

"Yes," was the answer. "You need't look for him, I gave him the money."

"You gave him the money! What money?" exclaimed Mrs. Bobbsey. "I didn't send him for any money."

"Why, I saw him come out of your room and start for the elevator," the maid went on. "I was working across the hall. I heard your little boy saying that he couldn't get in without money and then he looked at me. He asked me if I had eleven cents and I gave it to him."

"You gave my little boy Freddie eleven cents?" asked Mrs. Bobbsey wondering if it were all a joke. "Why did you do that?"

"Because he said he wanted it to get into the moving picture place just down the street," the chambermaid said. "I thought you had let him go, and that he had forgotten the money. It's ten cents for children to get in afternoons, you know, and a penny for war tax. I gave it to him."

"Dear me!" exclaimed Mrs. Bobbsey. "The

idea of his doing that! Which moving picture place was it?"

"I know!" broke in Bert. "It must be the one we were in yesterday where they had the cowboy and Indian scenes. Freddie has gone there again."

"He did want to see an Indian," added Nan.

"But would they let such a little boy in all alone?" asked Mrs. Bobbsey.

"Oh, lots of the children get grown-ups to take them in," the chambermaid explained. "I've often seen 'em do it."

"But I don't want Freddie going by himself or with people he doesn't know!" said the little boy's mother. "But it was kind of you to give him the money, and here is your change back," she said to the hotel maid. "But now we must get Freddie."

"I'll get him," offered Bert. "I know just where the place is."

"I wish you would," returned Mrs. Bobbsey. "Bring him right back here. I shall have to scold him a little."

Bert went down in the elevator. The man running the big wire cage, which lifted people up and down instead of having them go by the stairs, nodded and smiled at Bert.

"I took yo' little brother down awhile ago," said the elevator man, who was colored like Sam Johnson.

"Yes, he ran away," replied Bert.

"Guess you'll find him at de movies!" laughed the elevator man. "He had 'leven cents, an' he was talkin' 'bout Indians an' cowboys."

"Yes, he's crazy about 'em," answered Bert "We're going out West you know."

"Is you?" asked the man, as the elevator went down. "Well, de West am a mighty big place. I suah hopes yo' l'il brother doan git lost in de big West."

"We'll have to keep watch over him," returned Bert, as he got out of the car and hurried down the street toward the moving picture theater. On the way he was wondering as to the best way of getting Freddie out of the show. It would be dark inside, Bert knew, though the picture on the screen made it light at times. But it would be too dark to pick Freddie out of the crowd, especially as the theater was a large place and Bert did not know where his small brother would be sitting.

"I guess I'll have to speak to the girl that sells tickets, and maybe she can tell me how to find Freddie," thought Bert.

But when he reached the moving picture theater he had no trouble at all. For Freddie was there, and he was outside, and not inside at all. And the reason Freddie had not gone in was for the same reason that a number of other boys and girls were standing outside the theater.

In the lobby, or the open place near the ticket window, stood a tall man, wearing a red shirt, a big hat with a leather band on it, and, around his neck, a large purple handkerchief. The man wore big boots, and his trousers, instead of being of cloth as were those of Bert's father, were made of sheepskin.

"Oh, he's a cowboy!" exclaimed Bert. And so the man was. At least he was dressed as some cowboys dress, especially in moving pictures, and this man was standing in front of the theater to advertise the photoplay and draw a crowd.

The crowd was there, and Freddie was right up in front, looking with open eyes and open mouth at the cowboy, who was walking back and forth, letting himself be looked at.

"Freddie! Freddie!" called Bert, when he had worked his way close to his little brother. "What you doing here?"

"I'm going to the show!" declared Freddie. "I want to see the wild cows again. And look, Bert! Here's a cowboy like those we're going to see a lot of when we get out West!"

Freddie spoke so loudly that many in the crowd laughed, as did the cowboy himself. Then as the big man in the red shirt and sheepskin trousers happened to remember that he was there to advertise the show he began saying:

"Step right inside, ladies and gentlemen, and boys and girls. See the big cattle round-up and the Indian raid! Step in and see the cowboys taming the wild horses!"

"Come on in!" called Freddie to Bert. "I want to see it! I want to see the show! I've 'leven cents! The lady in the hotel gave it to me!"

"No, you can't go in now!" said Bert firmly, as he kept hold of his little brother's hand. "Mother want you. She didn't like it because you ran away. We thought maybe vou fell out the window."

"But I didn't!" cried Freddie. "I came down in the levelator, and I want to see the show."

"Not now," said Bert kindly, as he led Freddie out of the crowd. "Mother is going to take us all down town to buy things."

"But I want to see the show!" insisted Freddie, and he was going to cry, Bert feared, when there appeared, out in front of the hotel, an Italian with a hurdy-gurdy.

Freddie was always ready to look at something like this, and soon he was in the crowd listening to the man grind out the tunes.

"I'm going to give him this penny," said Freddie, showing the coins the chambermaid had given him. "I'll keep the ten cents, and maybe I can get another penny to go to the movies. But I'll give the man this one."

"All right," agreed Bert, glad enough to get Freddie away from the cowboy. And ther

Freddie seemed to forget all about wanting to go to the movies in listening to the music.

By this time Mrs. Bobbsey, Nan and Flossie had come down from their rooms. They saw Bert and Freddie in the crowd around the hurdy-gurdy man.

"Oh, I'm glad you have found him!" exclaimed Freddie's mother, as she saw her little son. "You did very wrong to run away," she added.

Freddie looked sorry, for he knew he was being scolded.

"I—I didn't go into the movies," he said, "and I have ten cents left. I gave a penny to the man," and he showed his mother the ten-cent piece in his chubby fist.

"You must never do such a thing again, Freddie," went on Mrs. Bobbsey. "Now I'm going to take that ten cents away from you, and when you want to go to the movies you must ask me."

"Will you take me to see the cowboy after we go shopping?" the little fellow wanted to know.

"I don't believe we'll have time," Mrs.

Bobbsey answered, trying not to smile. "We must get ready to leave for Lumberville then."

"Oh, that'll be fun!" cried Freddie. "I want to see the big trees. Maybe I'll climb one."

"And that's something else you must not do!" went on his mother. "You must not go out in the woods nor climb trees alone."

"I won't. Bert will come with me," said Freddie.

Then the Bobbsey twins went shopping with their mother, and that night they again got aboard a sleeping car and started for Lumberville, which was reached the next morning.

And when Flossie and Freddie and Bert and Nan opened their eyes and looked from the car window they saw a strange sight.

CHAPTER XIII

THE SAWMILL

WHEN Bert, who was the first of the Bobbsey twins to awaken, looked from the car window he had hard work to tell whether or not he was dreaming. For he seemed to be traveling through a scene from a moving picture. There were trees, trees, trees on both sides of the track. Nothing could be seen but trees. The railroad was cut through a dense forest, and at times the trees seemed so near that it appeared all Bert would have to do would be to stretch out his hand to touch the branches.

Then Nan awakened, and she, too, saw the great numbers of trees on both sides of the train. Quickly she and Bert dressed, and, finding a place where a sleeping berth had been folded up and the seats made ready for use again, the two children took their places there and looked out.

"What makes so many trees?" asked Nan. "Is this a camping place?"

"It would be a dandy place for us Boy Scouts to camp," said Bert. "But I guess this must be where they get lumber from, isn't it, Daddy?" he asked, as his father came through the car just then, having been to the wash-room to shave.

"Yes, this is the place of big trees and lumber," said Mr. Bobbsey. "We are coming to Lumberville soon, and half our journey will be over."

"Is this the West?" asked Nan.

"Yes, this is the West," her father told her, "though it is not as far West as we are going. The cattle ranch is still farther on. It will take us some time to get there, but we are going to stay in Lumberville nearly a week."

By this time Flossie and Freddie had awakened and their mother had helped them to dress. The two smaller Bobbsey twins came to sit with Nan and Bert and look out of the windows.

"My, what a lot of trees!" exclaimed Freddie.

"You couldn't climb all them, could you?" asked Flossie.

"Not all at once, but I could climb one at a time," Freddie answered, as the train puffed on through the forest. "Can't we stop in the woods?" he wanted to know. "These are terrible big woods."

"Yes, this is a large forest," said Mr. Bobbsey. "It is one of the largest in the United States, and some of my lumber and boards come from here. But we can't stop here. If we did we would have no nice hot breakfast."

"Oh, then I don't want to stop!" exclaimed Freddie. "I'm hungry."

"We'll soon have breakfast," said his mother. "It is wonderful among the trees," she said. "And to think that I will really own a tract of woodland like this!"

"Yes," replied Mr. Bobbsey. "Your lumber tract will be much like this, except there will be places where trees have been cut down to be made into boards and planks. I suppose there are such places in these woods, but we cannot see them from the train."

Once, just before they went into the dining car to breakfast, the Bobbsey twins saw in a clearing a big wagon loaded with logs and drawn by eight horses.

"Oh, look!" cried Bert, pointing to it. "Will you have teams like that, Mother?"

"Well, I suppose so," she answered. "I don't really know what is on my lumber tract, as yet."

"We'll soon see," said Mr. Bobbsey, looking at his watch. "We'll be at Lumberville in about two hours."

They went to breakfast while the train was still puffing along through the woods. The scenery was quite different from that on the first part of their journey, where they had scarcely ever been out of sight of houses and cities, with only now and then a patch of wooded land. Here there were hardly any houses to be seen—only trees, trees, and more trees.

Freddie was not the only one of the Bobbsey twins who was hungry, for Flossie, Nan, and

Bert also had good appetites. But, to tell you the truth, the children were more interested in looking out of the window than in eating, though they did not miss much that was on the table.

Mr. and Mrs. Bobbsey were glad they had brought the twins along, for they felt the trip would do them good and let the children see things they never would have seen but for the travel.

After they had gone back into the sleeping car, where the berths had all been folded up against the roof by this time, Mr. Bobbsey said they had better begin getting their baggage ready.

"The train does not stop long at Lumberville, and we must hurry out," he said. "Lumberville isn't a big, city station, like the one in Chicago."

"Are there any moving pictures there?" Freddie wanted to know.

"No, not a one," his mother answered. "But there will be plenty of other things for you to see."

Soon after the satchels, baskets, and bundles

belonging to the Bobbsey twins had been gathered together by the car porter and put at the end, near the door, the train began to run more slowly.

"Is this Lumberville?" asked Bert, who had noticed that the trees were not quite so thick now.

"Lumberville—Lumber-ville!" called the porter, smiling back at the Bobbsey twins as he stood near their pile of baggage. "All out for Lumberville."

"That's us!" cried Bert, with a laugh.

Slowly the train came to a stop. Bert and Nan, standing near the window from which they had been looking all the morning, saw a small, rough building flash into view. Near it were flatcars piled high with lumber and logs. But there was no sign of a city or a town.

"Come on!" called Daddy Bobbsey to his family.

The porter carried out their baggage, and the children jumped down the car steps. They found themselves on the platform of a small station—a station that looked more like a shanty in the woods than a place for railroad trains to stop.

"Good-bye! An' good luck to yo' all!" called the smiling porter, as he climbed up the car steps, carrying the rubber-covered stool he had put down for the passengers to alight on.

Then the train puffed away and the Bobbsey twins, with their father and mother, and with their baggage around them, stood on the platform of the station which, as Bert could see, was marked "Lumberville."

"But where's the place? Where's the town? Where's the men cutting down trees and all that?" Bert asked. He was beginning to feel disappointed.

"Oh, this is only where the trains stop," his father said. "Lumberville isn't a city, or even a town. It's just a settlement for the lumbermen. Our timber tract is about seven miles from here."

"Have we got to walk?" asked Nan, as she looked down at her dainty, new shoes which her mother had bought in Chicago.

"No, we don't have to walk. I think this

is our automobile coming now," replied Mr. Bobbsey, and he smiled at his wife.

Bert and Nan heard a rumbling sound back of the rough, wooden railroad station. Flossie and Freddie were too busy watching and listening to some blue jays in a tree overhead to pay attention to much else. But as the rumbling sound grew louder Bert saw a big wagon approaching, drawn by two powerful horses.

"Where's the automobile?" asked the boy, with a look at his father.

"I was just joking," said Mr. Bobbsey. "The roads here are too rough for autos. Lumber wagons are about all that can get through."

"Are we going in that wagon?" Nan demanded.

Before her father could answer the man driving the big horses called to them to stop, and when they did he spoke to Mr. Bobbsey.

"Are you the folks I'm expected to take out to the Watson timber tract?" the driver asked.

"Well, we are the Bobbseys," said Bert's father

"Then you're the folks I want!" was the good-natured answer. "Just pile in and make yourselves comfortable. I'll get your baggage in."

"I'd better help you," said Mr. Bobbsey. "There's quite a lot of it."

"Oh, we're going to have a ride!" cried Freddie as he ran over to the lumber wagon, followed by Flossie. "This is better than an automobile."

"Well, it's more sure, over the roads we've got to travel," said the driver, who was carrying two valises while Mr. Bobbsey took two more to put in the wagon.

"Pile in!" invited the driver again, and when the Bobbsey twins reached the wagon they found it was half-filled with pine tree branches, over which horse blankets had been spread.

"Why, it's as soft as a sleeping car!" exclaimed Nan. "Oh, how nice this is!" and she sank down with a sigh of contentment.

Bert helped Flossie and Freddie in, and Mr. Bobbsey helped in his wife.

"Got everything?" asked the driver, as he

CHAPTER XIV

THE BIG TREE

THE Bobbsey twins saw, just ahead of them, a stream of water sparkling in the sun. They also saw a place that had been cleared of trees, which had been cut down, making a vacant place in the woods. And in this clearing, or vacant place, near the small river, were a number of rough-looking buildings. It was from one of these "shacks," as Bert afterward called them, that the screeching sound came. And puffs of steam coming from a pipe sticking out of the roof of this shack showed that there was an engine there.

"Is this the lumber camp that I am to own?" asked Mrs. Bobbsey, as she looked ahead and saw the buildings, the piles of logs, and the stacks of boards.

"This is the place," said Mr. Bobbsey. "It is bigger than I thought. We will have to get some one to look after it for you, Mother. You and I can't be running out here to see that the men cut down the trees right, and make them into boards. Yes, we shall have to get some one to help us."

"Couldn't I help?" asked Bert. "Maybe I'd rather be a lumberman than a cowboy."

"You'll have to grow some before you'll be of much use around a lumber camp," said the driver of the wagon. "It's hard work chopping down trees."

"Do you ever have a fire here?" Freddie demanded suddenly.

"Sometimes, my little man," the driver answered. "Why? Do you like to see fires? I don't, myself, for they burn up a lot of good lumber."

"I don't like to see fires, but I like fire engines," said Freddie. "And I have a fire engine at home, and it squirts real water. But I couldn't bring it with me 'cause it was too heavy to carry. But if there was a fire here maybe I could watch the engines—I mean the big ones."

"We don't have fire engines in lumber

camps," said the driver, whose name was Harvey Hallock. "When it starts to burn we just have to let her burn. But I guess—"

However, no one heard what he said, for at that moment the saw must have come to another hard knot in a log, for there was that same loud screeching sound like a wild animal yelling.

Nan covered her ears with her hands, but Bert and Freddie and Flossie seemed to like the noise.

"Mercy me!" exclaimed Mrs. Bobbsey, "I hope that doesn't happen very often."

"Well, I might as well tell you it does," said Mr. Hallock. "We keep the sawmill going all day, but of course we shut down at night. It won't keep you awake, anyhow."

"That's good," said Mrs. Bobbsey, with a laugh. "I don't believe I'd want to own a lumber saw if it kept me awake with a noise like that."

Certainly this sawmill in the midst of the big lumber tract was very different from the small one in Mr. Bobbsey's place at Lakeport. The children often watched the men sawing up boards at the yard their father owned, but the work there was nothing like this.

The saw cut through the hard knot and the screeching sound came to an end, at least for a time.

"This is where you folks are going to stay," said Mr. Hallock, as he stopped his team in front of a building, at the sight of which Bert and Nan gave shouts of joy.

"It's a regular log cabin! Oh, it's a regular log cabin!" cried Bert, as he saw where they were to live during their stay in the lumber camp.

"So this is to be our cabin, is it?" said Mr. Bobbsey as he got down and helped his wife, while the driver lifted out the children and then the baggage.

"Yes, the boys fixed this up for you," answered Mr. Hallock. "We hope you'll like it."

"I'm sure I shall," said Mrs. Bobbsey, as she looked inside the log cabin, for it really was that, the sides being made of logs piled one on the other, the ends being notched so they would not slip out.

"Isn't it cute!" exclaimed Nan, as she followed her mother inside the cabin. "It has tables and chairs and a cupboard and everything!"

"And it's all made of wood!" cried Bert. "Say, the Boy Scouts would like this all right."

"I believe they would," agreed his father. "As for everything being made of wood, it generally is in a lumber camp. Now we must get settled. Where can I find the foreman?" he asked of the driver of the wagon who had brought the Bobbseys over from the railroad station.

"He's outside somewhere in the woods," was the answer. "I'll find him and tell him you're here. I'll send the cook over to see if he can get you anything to eat. Are you hungry?" he asked the children.

"I am!" admitted Bert.

"And so am I!"

"And I!" echoed Flossie and Freddie.

"Well, that's the way to be!" said Mr. Hallock. "Children wouldn't be children unless they were hungry. We've got plenty to eat here, such as it is. Not much pie and cake, perhaps, but other things."

"We don't want pie and cake when we're camping in the woods," declared Bert. "We didn't have it at Blueberry Island—that is, not every day."

"All right! I guess you'll get along!" laughed the driver, as he went off through the trees to find the cook and some of the men of the lumber camp.

Mr. and Mrs. Bobbsey were looking about the log cabin that was to be their home for about a week, and the children were playing about outside, watching some squirrels and chipmunks that were frisking about in the trees, when a voice called:

"Well, I see you got here all right!"

Mr. Bobbsey and his wife, who were putting some of their baggage in one of the inner rooms, came to the outside door. They saw a big bearded man, wearing heavy boots, with his trousers tucked in the tops of them, smiling at them."

"Are you the foreman?" asked Mr. Bobbsey.

"No, I'm Tom Jackson, his helper," was the answer. "Mr. Dayton will be over in a few minutes. He's seeing about some big trees that are being cut down."

"I don't want to take him away from his work," said Mr. Bobbsey.

"Oh, he's coming over, anyhow, to see how you stood the trip out to this rough place," said Mr. Jackson. "Of course it isn't as rough as it is in the winter time, when we do most of our tree-cutting, but it's rough enough, even now."

"We are used to roughing it," said Mrs. Bobbsey, with a smile. "We like it, and the children think there is no better fun than camping out."

"Well, that's what this is—camping out," said the foreman's helper. "But here comes the cook, and he looks as if he had something for you to eat."

A little bald-headed man, with a white apron draped in front of him, was coming along a woodland path with some covered dishes on a tray held on one hand, while in the other he carried what seemed to be a coffee pot.

"Just brought you folks some sandwiches and a pot of tea," he said, as he set the things down on the table in the log cabin. "This is tea even if it's made in the coffee pot. But I washed it out good first," he said to Mrs. Bobbsey. "Mostly the lumber men like coffee, though in winter they're fond of a hot cup of tea. I give 'em both, and generally I have a teapot, but I can't find it just this minute. I brought some fried cakes for the children, too."

"I thought he said there wasn't any cake in a lumber camp," said Bert, looking out toward the driver who was going off with his team.

"Well, generally I don't get much time to make fried cakes," said the little bald-headed man who acted as cook. "But I made some specially for you youngsters to-day," and he lifted off the cover of one dish and showed some crisp, brown doughnuts, which he called "fried cakes."

"Oh, I want some!" cried Freddie.

So do I!" echoed Flossie.

"There's enough for all of you," remarked the cook. "Now, then, Mrs. Bobbsey, you'll have a cup of tea, I know," and he poured out a hot, steaming cup that smelled very good.

Mr. Bobbsey ate some of the sandwiches and had a cup of tea, and, after they had taken the edge off their hunger on the doughnuts, the children also ate some of the bread and meat.

While their father and mother were talking to the assistant foreman and the cook, who said his name was Jed Prenty, the four Bobbsey twins wandered outside the log cabin. It stood on the edge of a clearing in the forest, and not far away there were other log buildings, most of them larger than the one where the Bobbseys were to live. These other buildings were where the lumbermen slept and ate, and one was where Jed Prenty did his cooking. In another building, farther off, the horses were stabled.

"Let's take a walk in the woods," said Bert to Nan. "I want to see 'em cut down trees."

"So do I," she said. "We can take Flossie and Freddie with us. We won't go far."

"Are there any cowboys here?" Freddie wanted to know.

"Not any, I guess," laughed Bert. "We'll

find them when we get to Cowdon, where mother's ranch is."

Before they knew it the Bobbsey twins had walked quite a little way along a path into the woods. They heard the sound of axes being used to chop down trees, and they were eager to see the lumbermen at work.

"Oh, look at this big tree!" called Freddie to Bert. "Some one cut it almost down!" He and Flossie had, for the moment, wandered away from Bert and Nan, though they were still within sight. At Freddie's call Bert looked up and toward his small brother.

Bert saw the two small Bobbsey twins standing beside a big tree which, as Freddie had said, was partly cut down. Just then came a puff of wind. The big tree slowly swayed and began to fall over. And Flossie and Freddie were standing near it, right where it would crash down on them!

CHAPTER XV

BILL DAYTON

"LOOK out there! Look out!"

Bert and Nan Bobbsey, standing near a big stump, heard some one shout this to Flossie and Freddie as the two small Bobbsey twins looked up at the great tree which was slowly falling toward them. And then Bert and Nan added their voices to the shout which came from they knew not whom.

"Oh, Flossie! Run! Run!" cried Nan.

"Come here, Freddie! Come here!" yelled Bert.

The two small children did not really know they were in danger. There was so much to see in the woods, and they were so interested in watching the big tree fall, that they did not know it might fall right on them and crush them.

"Oh, what shall we do? What shall we do?"

sobbed Nan, for she was crying now, for fear her little brother and sister would be hurt.

"I'll get 'em!" exclaimed Bert.

He started to run toward Flossie and Freddie, but he never could have reached them in time to snatch them out of the way of the falling tree.

However, there was some one else in the forest who knew just what to do and when to do it. There was another cry from some unseen man.

"Stand still! Don't move!" he shouted.

Then there was a crackling in the underbrush, and some one rushed out at Flossie and Freddie, who were standing under the tree looking up at the tottering trunk which was slowly falling toward them.

If the two little children had been alone in the woods they might have thought that the crackling and crashing in the underbrush was made by a bear breaking his way toward them. But they were not thinking of bears, just then.

In another instant Bert and Nan saw a man, dressed as were nearly all the "lumberjacks," spring down a little hill and rush at Flossie and Freddie. As for the two small Bobbsey twins themselves, they had no time to see anything very clearly. The first they knew they were caught up in the man's arms, Freddie on one side and Flossie on the other. That big, strong lumberman just tucked Freddie under his left arm and Flossie under his right and then he gave a jump and a leap that carried them all out of danger.

And only just in time, too! For no sooner had the lumberman picked up the two children and leaped off the path with them into a little cleared space than down crashed the big tree!

It made a sound like the boom of a big gun, or like the pounding of the giant waves in a storm at the seashore, where once the Bobbsey twins had spent a vacation.

Down crashed the big tree, breaking off smaller trees and bushes that were in its way. Down it fell, raising a big cloud of dust, and Flossie and Freddie, still held in the arms of the big man, saw it fall. But they were far enough away to escape getting hurt, though some pieces of bark and a shower of leaves scattered over them. The lumbermen had snatched them out of danger just in time.

"Oh! Oh! They're all right! They're saved!" gasped Nan, no longer crying now that she saw Flossie and Freddie were not hurt.

"Whew! That was pretty near a bad accident," said Bert, who had stopped running toward his brother and sister when he saw that the lumberman was going to get them.

As for the two little children themselves, they were so surprised at first that they did not know what to think. One moment they had been looking up at a big tree, wondering why it was toppling over toward them as they had sometimes seen their tall towers of building blocks fall. The next instant they had heard somebody rushing toward them out of the woods, they had felt themselves caught up in strong arms, and now they were being set down at a safe distance away from the fallen tree by a big man.

Flossie and Freddie looked at the big trunk which had crashed down. Then they saw Bert and Nan coming toward them. Next they looked up at the big lumberman.

"Who are you?" asked Freddie.

"That's just what I was going to ask you," replied the big man, with a laugh. "I think I can guess, though. You are the Bobbsey twins, aren't you? That is you're half of them, and the other half is over there," and he pointed to Bert and Nan who were walking toward Flossie and Freddie.

"Yes, we're the Bobbsey twins," answered Freddie. "We've come to the lumber camp. My mother—she owns it."

"So I've heard," the man said. "Well, if I were you I wouldn't go off by myself among the trees again. You never can tell when one is going to fall down. The man who cut this one should have stayed and finished it, and not have left it to fall with the first puff of wind. I must speak to him about it. And now I had better take you to your father and mother. Where are they?"

"We'll take them back, thank you," said Nan, who, with Bert, came up just then.

"Yes, we want to thank you a lot for getting

them out of the way of the falling tree," went on Bert.

"It was the only way to save them," replied the lumberman. "I couldn't make them understand they must step back out of danger, so I had to rush to them and grab them. I'm afraid I did it pretty roughly, but I didn't mean to."

"You pinched me a little," said Flossie, speaking for the first time. "But I don't care. I wouldn't want that tree to hit me."

"I should say not!" exclaimed the lumberman. "We don't want the Bobbsey twins to get hurt."

"How'd you know our names are Bobbsey?" asked Freddie. "Are you a policeman? If you are, where's your brass buttons?"

"No, I'm not a policeman," answered the lumberman. "I suppose, in the city where you came from, all the policemen know you. But I guessed who you were because I sent a man to the depot to-day to meet the Bobbsey family, and you must belong to it."

"We do," explained Bert. "Our father and

mother are back in the camp—at the log cabin, you know."

"Yes, I know where it is very well," said the man, with a smile. "And, just to make sure you children won't go near any other trees that are ready to fall, I'll go back with you. I want to see Mr. and Mrs. Bobbsey, anyhow."

"Do you work here?" asked Bert.

"Yes, I think you could call it that," answered the man, with a smile.

He took Flossie and Freddie by the hands, and they walked along with him, while Bert and Nan followed. On the way back to the camp, or place where the log cabins and other shacks were built, they met a man coming along with an axe on his shoulder.

"That big tree fell down," said the man who had saved the Bobbsey twins. "After this don't go away and leave a trunk nearly chopped through. These children might have been hurt."

"I'm sorry," said the man with the axe. "I won't do it again. But, just as I was going to finish chopping it down, one of the boys needed help with his team, and I ran to him. I forgot all about the big tree."

"Well, don't forget again," said the man who had saved Flossie and Freddie.

As the Bobbseys walked along with their new friend they saw their father and mother coming toward them.

"Bert, Nan, where have you been?" asked their mother.

"Off in the woods," Bert answered.

"And we saw a big tree fall down and it 'most falled on us!" added Flossie.

"But he pulled us out from under it! Didn't you?" went on Freddie, and he looked up at the big man in the big boots, who wore a red shirt like the other lumbermen.

"What's that?" asked Mr. Bobbsey. "Were you children near a falling tree?"

"That's what they were—too near for comfort," said the man as he let go of the hands of Flossie and Freddie, so the small Bobbsey twins might run to their mother. "It was careless of one of the men to leave a tree half chopped through. But no harm is done. I managed to get the kiddies out of the way in time."

Mr. Bobbsey must have guessed how it happened, for he shook hands heartily with the lumberman.

"I can't thank you enough," said the children's father. "You saved Flossie and Freddie from being hurt, if not killed! Do you work here?"

"I'm the foreman," answered the man quietly.

"Oh, we have been looking for you," said Bert's mother. "I am Mrs. Bobbsey."

"That's what I guessed, lady," answered the man. "I am glad to meet you. I've been expecting you."

"So you are the foreman," said Mr. Bobbsey slowly. "May I ask your name?"

The man seemed to wait a few seconds before answering. Then he looked away over the tops of the trees and said:

"Bill Dayton."

And his voice sounded rather strange, Mrs. Bobbsey thought.

CHAPTER XVI

THE TRAIN CRASH

"WELL, Mr. Dayton," said Mr. Bobbsey, after a moment's pause, "as I said before, I do not know how to thank you for what you did to save Flossie and Freddie. I hope, some day, I may be able to do you as great a service as you did me."

And the time was nearer than Mr. Bobbsey supposed when he could do a kindness to the lumber foreman.

They all walked back to the log cabin near the other buildings, all of which made what was called the "lumber camp." The story was told of the falling tree, and how nearly Flossie and Freddie had been caught under it.

"That foreman of ours sure is quick on his feet!" said Harvey Hallock, the driver who had brought the Bobbseys from the station. Mr. Hallock was speaking to Mr. Bobbsey, outside the log cabin. "Yes, Bill Dayton is sure a quick man," went on the driver.

"Has he been foreman here long?" asked Mr. Bobbsey.

"No, not very long," was the answer. "He came here when your wife's uncle owned the tract, just before the uncle died. But we don't know much about Bill Dayton. He's a quiet man, and he doesn't talk much."

"I thought there was something queer about him," said Mr. Bobbsey. "But I shall always be his friend, for he saved my two children."

The Bobbsey twins thought they never had eaten such a jolly meal as the one served a little later in the log cabin. Even though it was in the midst of a great forest and in a lumber camp, the food was very good. The little bald-headed cook seemed to know almost as much as did black Dinah about making things taste good.

"The children have good appetites up here," said Mr. Bobbsey, as he filled Bert's plate for the second time.

"I want some, too!" called Freddie. "I'm hungry like a bear!"

"But you musn't eat like a bear!" said his mother, laughing. "You must wait your turn," and she served Flossie first, for that little "fairy" was as hungry as the others.

"What funny little beds!" exclaimed Nan, when she saw where they were to sleep in the log cabin.

"They're almost like the berths in the sleeping car," said Bert.

"They are called 'bunks,'" his father told him. "Lumbermen move about so, from camp to camp, that they could not take regular beds with them. So they build bunks against the wall, spreading their blankets over pine or hemlock boughs, as the driver did in the wagon we rode over in from the station."

But the bunks in the log cabin had mattresses stuffed with straw, and though they were not like the beds in the Pullman car, nor like those in the Bobbsey home, all the children slept well.

They did not awaken all night, nor did Freddie fall out of bed, as sometimes happened.

"I never slept so well in all my life!" exclaimed Mother Bobbsey, when she was getting ready for breakfast the next morning. "The sweet air of the lumber camp seems to agree with all of us."

Bert and Nan, as well as Flossie and Freddie, also felt fine, and they were ready for a day of fun. They had it, too, for there were so many things to do in the big tract of trees their mother now owned that the children did not know what to start first.

Of course Mr. and Mrs. Bobbsey had business to look after—the business of taking over the lumber camp, since Mrs. Bobbsey was now the owner. But she made no changes. She said she wanted Bill Dayton still to act as foreman, and she wished to keep the same men he had hired from the first, as he said they were all good workers.

But while their father and mother were in the office of the lumber camp, looking over books and papers, Bert and Nan and Flossie and Freddie roamed about. They did not go alone, as that would not have been safe. Harvey Hallock, the good-natured driver of the wagon, went with them, and foreman Bill Dayton told him to be especially careful not to let Flossie and Freddie stray away.

"I guess he thinks I'll get lost," said Freddie, when the little "fireman" heard this order given to the driver.

"Do you often get lost?" asked Harvey Hallock.

"Oh, lots of times!" exclaimed Freddie. "I can get lost as easy as anything! But I always get found again!"

"Well, that's good!" laughed the driver.

He took the children to the sawmill, and, at a safe distance from the big saw, they watched to see how logs were turned into boards, planks, and beams.

They saw the rumbling wagons drive up, loaded with logs that were fastened on with chains so they would not roll off. The men, with big hooks fastened on handles of wood, turned the logs over, and slid them this way and that until they could be shoved up to the saw.

The logs were put on what was called a "carriage," to be sawed. This carriage moved slowly along on a little track, and the Bobbsey twins were allowed to ride on the end of the log farthest from the saw. When the end came too close to the big, whirring teeth that ripped through the hard knots with such a screaching sound, Bert and Nan and Flossie and Freddie were lifted off by the driver.

The children saw the place where the jolly, bald-headed cook made the meals ready for the hungry men. There was a big stove, and on it a pot of soup was cooking, and when Jed Prenty opened the oven door a most delicious smell came out.

"What's that?" asked Bert.

'Baked beans," the cook answered. "They're 'most done, too! Want some?"

"Oh, I do!" cried Freddie. "And I want a fried cake, too!"

"So do I!" echoed Flossie.

"Well, you shall have some," answered the good-natured cook. So he gave the children a little lunch on one end of the big, long table where the lumbermen would soon crowd in to dinner.

The Bobbsey twins had no fear of "spoiling their appetites" by eating thus before their regular lunch was ready. Walking about in the woods seemed to make them hungry all the while.

As the days passed Mrs. Bobbsey found she would have to stay in Lumberville longer than she had at first thought. There was much business to be done in taking over the property her uncle had left her.

"The longer we stay the better I like it!" said Nan to Bert. "There are so many birds here, and squirrels and chipmunks. And the squirrels are so tame that they come right up to me."

"Yes, they are nice," said Bert. "But I want to get out West on the ranch, and see the cowboys and the Indians."

"I want to be an Indian, too!" exclaimed Freddie, who did not quite catch what Bert said.

"What else do you want to be?" laughed the older brother. "First you're going to be a fireman, and now you want to be an Indian!"

"Couldn't I be both?" Freddie wanted to know.

"Hardly," said Nan, with a laugh. "You'd

better just stay what you are—Freddie Bobbsey!"

Day after day the twins were taken around the woods by the driver or some of the lumbermen who were not busy. They saw big trees cut down, but were careful not to get in the way of the great, swaying trunks. They played in the piles of sawdust, jumping off powdery wood.

"This is as nice as Blueberry Island!" cried Nan one day, when they were all playing on the sawdust heap.

"Yes, and we're having as much fun as we did in Washington, where we found Miss Pompret's china," added Bert. "I wonder if we'll discover any mystery on this trip."

"I don't believe so," returned Nan.

However, the Bobbsey twins were to help in solving something which you will read about before this book is finished.

But all things have an end, even the happy days in the lumber camp, and one morning, after the little bald-headed cook had served breakfast in the log cabin, Mr. Bobbsey said to the children:

"Well, we are going to travel on."

"Where are we going?" asked Bert.

"To Cowdon; to the cattle ranch," answered Mrs. Bobbsey. "I have settled all the business here, and now we must go farther out West."

"I'll be sorry to see you go," said the foreman, Bill Dayton, when told that the Bobbseys were going to leave. "I've enjoyed the children very much."

"Did you ever have any of your own?" asked Mr. Bobbsey.

"No—never did," was the answer. "I'm not much of a family man. Used to be, when I was a boy and lived at home," he went on. "But that's a good many years ago."

"Haven't you any family—any relatives?" asked Mrs. Bobbsey, for she thought the foreman spoke as if he were very lonesome.

"Well, yes, I've got some folks," answered Bill Dayton slowly. "I've got a brother somewhere out West. He's a cowboy, I believe. Haven't seen him for some years."

"Are your father and mother dead?" asked Mr. Bobbsey gently.

"My mother is," was the answer. "She died

when my brother and I were boys. As for my father—well, I don't talk much about him," and the foreman turned away as if that ended it.

"Why doesn't he want to talk about his father?" asked Bert of Mr. Bobbsey a little later, when they were packing the valises.

"I don't know," was the answer. "Perhaps he and his father quarreled, or something like that. We had better not ask too many questions. Bill Dayton is a queer man."

Bert thought so himself, but he did as his father had suggested, and did not ask the foreman any more questions.

The packing was soon finished, and then the Bobbsey twins said good-bye to their friends in the lumber camp. The bald-headed cook gave them a bag of "fried cakes" to take with them. They were to ride to the station in the same lumber wagon that had brought them to the camp, and Harvey Hallock was to drive them.

"Good-bye!" said Bill Dayton to Mr. and Mrs. Bobbsey, after he had talked to the Bobbsey twins. "If you stop off here on your way home from your ranch, we'll all be glad to see you."

"Perhaps we may stop off," Mrs. Bobbsey answered. "Now that I own a lumber tract I must look after it, though I am going to leave the management of it to you."

"I'll do my best with it," promised the foreman. "And if you should happen to meet my brother out among the cowboys tell him I was asking for him. I don't s'pose you will meet him, but you might."

And then the Bobbsey twins started off on another part of their trip to the great West. They did not have long to wait for the train in the Lumberville station, and, as they got aboard and began their travels once more, they could see Harvey Hallock waving to them from his wagon.

"And one of the horses shook his head good-bye to me!" exclaimed Flossie, who pressed her chubby nose against the window to catch the last view of the lumber team.

"I hope we have as good a time on the cattle ranch as we had in the lumber camp," said

Nan, as she and the other children settled down for the long ride.

"We'll have more fun!" declared Bert. "We can ride ponies out on the ranch!"

"Oh, may we?" asked Nan with shining eyes, turning to her mother.

"I guess so," was the answer.

"I want a pony, too!" cried Freddie. "If Bert and Nan ride pony-back Flossie and I want to ride, too."

"We'll ride you in a little cart," said Mr. Bobbsey, with a laugh. "That will be safer—you won't fall so easily."

They were to ride all that day, all night, and part of the next day before they would reach the cattle ranch which Mrs. Bobbsey's uncle had left her. The railroad trip was enjoyed by the Bobbseys, but the children were eager to get to the new place they were going to visit. Bert wanted to see the cowboys and the Indians, Nan wanted to ride a pony and get an Indian doll, and as for Flossie and Freddie, they just wanted to have a good time in any way possible.

Supper was served on the train, and then

came the making up of the berths in the sleeping car. This was nothing new to the Bobbseys now, and soon they were all in bed.

It was dark and about the middle of the night when all in the sleeping car were suddenly awakened by a loud crash. The train stopped with a jerk, there was a shrieking of whistles, and then loud shouts.

"What is it?" called Mrs. Bobbsey from her berth.

"Probably there has been a wreck," said Mr. Bobbsey, as he quickly got out of his berth and into the aisle. "But no one here seems to be hurt, though I think the car is off the track."

Flossie and Freddie and Bert and Nan stuck their heads out between the curtains hanging in front of their berths. They wondered what had happened.

CHAPTER XVII

AT THE RANCH

After the first crash in the night, and the rattling and bumping of the sleeping car in which they were riding, the Bobbsey twins heard nothing more that was exciting except the whistling of the locomotive and the shouting of men outside the train.

But though the sleeping car no longer bumped unevenly over the wooden ties of the road bed, and though it had come to a stop, the people in it were all very much excited. Men and women quickly dressed, and came out in the aisle where Mr. and Mrs. Bobbsey were now standing.

"What is it?"

"What's the matter?"

"Are we off the track?"

These and many other questions were being asked by every one it seemed.

"I was dreamin' that I fell out of bed and I got a big bump!" said Freddie Bobbsey, and, hearing that, many of the passengers laughed.

This seemed to make them feel better, and when it was seen that the sleeping car was not broken and that no one in it was hurt, the men and women began to talk about what had best be done.

"We're off the track, that's sure," said one man who had a berth next to Mr. Bobbsey. "You can tell we're off the track by the way this car is tipped to one side."

"Yes, I believe we are," said the children's father. "Well, if it isn't anything worse than being off the track we will not worry much. But there was a pretty hard crash, and I'm afraid some of the passengers in the other cars are hurt."

"You're right—it was a hard crash," said a woman to whom Mrs. Bobbsey was speaking. "It awakened me from a sound sleep. If we are off the track I wonder how long it will take us to get back on?"

"I have a train of cars," said Freddie, who, with the other Bobbsey children, was now partly dressed. "I have a train of cars, and when they get off the track Flossie and I put 'em back on."

"Well, I wish you could do that with this train, my little engineer!" laughed the man who had talked to Freddie's father.

"I'm not an engineer!" exclaimed the little fellow, smiling.

"No?" asked the man.

"Nope! I'm a fireman, and my sister's a fairy!" went on Freddie, pointing to Flossie so every one would know he did not mean Nan.

"Well, if she is a fairy maybe she can wave her magic wand and put us all back on the track again," went on the man. "Can you do that, little fairy?" he asked. "Where is your magic wand?"

"I—I hasn't any," answered Flossie, who was feeling a bit shy and bashful because so many persons were looking at her and smiling.

"Well, here comes the conductor," said some one. "Perhaps he can tell us what the matter is, even if he can't put the train back on the rails. What's wrong, conductor?" asked a man whose hair was all tousled from having gotten out of his berth in such a hurry.

"There has been an accident," explained the train conductor. "It isn't a bad one, but it will hold us here for an hour or two."

"Is any one hurt?" asked Mrs. Bobbsey.

"No, I'm glad to say no one is," the conductor said. "Our train ran into a freight car that stuck too far over the edge of its own track out on our track. Our engine smashed the freight car, some damage was done to the locomotive itself, and the crash threw some of our cars off the rails. But no one was hurt more than being shaken up."

"That's good," said Mr. Bobbsey. "Then had we better stay right in our car?" he asked.

"Oh, yes," answered the conductor. "That's what I came in to tell you—stay right here. We have sent for the wrecking crew, and we will go on again as soon as we can. There is no danger. You need not be afraid, even if you get shaken up again."

"Are you going to shake us up?" asked Bert.

"No, but the wrecking crew will when they pull this car back on the rails," the conductor replied. "But don't be afraid—no one will be hurt."

The passengers quieted down after hearing this, and some of them who were good sleepers went back to bed. The Bobbsey twins were too wide-awake, their mother thought, to go to sleep so soon after the excitement, so she let them sit up a while to get quiet.

Going to the end of the car, in the little passageway near the wash room, Bert and Nan could look out of the window. They saw men with flaring oil torches hurrying here and there. These were the railroad workers getting ready to put the train back on the track.

There was not so much shouting, now that it was known no one was hurt, and soon the children heard the puffing of engines and the rumble of wheels.

"The wrecking crew has arrived," said Mr. Bobbsey, who came down the aisle to see if Bert and Nan were all right.

"What's a wrecking crew, Daddy?" asked Nan.

"They are the men who clear away wrecked trains," her father answered. "Don't you remember? You saw them at the wreck in our town."

"Oh, yes!" exclaimed Nan. "There was one car with a big derrick on it, and it lifted the broken pieces of the wrecked cars out of the way."

"That's the wreck Mr. Hickson was hurt in," went on Bert. "I guess his wreck was worse than this one."

"Yes, it was," said Mr. Bobbsey. "All railroad wrecks are bad enough, but some are worse than others. But now I think you children had better get back to your berths. There isn't much more to see. You can feel the rest."

"You mean we can feel the bumping when they put us back on the rails?" asked Bert.

"Yes," his father told him.

And a little while after Bert and his sister had got back in their berths they did feel a rumbling and bumping. There were more shouts out in the darkness of the night, and, peering under the edges of their curtains, the children saw more flickering torches and moving men.

Then came an extra big bump, and the sleeping car swayed from side to side. A moment later it began to roll along smoothly.

"I guess we're back on the track now," said Bert.

"Yes," his father answered, "we are. Now we'll travel along."

And in about two hours after the wreck the train was on its journey again, not much the worse for the accident. The freight car had been smashed and so had the front part of the passenger engine. But another locomotive had come with the wrecking train, and this was used to haul the Bobbseys and other passengers where they wanted to go.

"Now we'll have something to tell Mr. Hickson when we get back home," said Bert to Nan the next morning at the breakfast table.

"You mean about the wreck?" asked Nan.

"Yes," replied Bert. "Course ours wasn't a big wreck, like his, but it was big enough."

"I don't want another," said Nan. "I like Mr. Hickson; don't you, Bert?"

"Yes, I do. And I wish we could find his two sons for him, but I don't s'pose we can."

"No," agreed Nan, "we can't ever do that."

It was about noon on the day after the night of the wreck, that Mr. Bobbsey said to his wife and children:

"We will get out soon."

"Shall we be in Cowdon?" asked Bert. "At the ranch?"

"No, not exactly at the ranch," his father told him. "But we'll reach the town of Cowdon, and from there we'll drive to the ranch, which is about ten miles from the railroad."

"Oh, may I ride a pony out to the ranch?" cried Bert.

"I don't believe they'll bring any ponies to meet us," said Mr. Bobbsey. "Later on you may ride one."

The train pulled into the little western station. Some time since the big stretches of woods and trees had been left behind, and now the Bobbseys were in the open prairie country—the land of cattle, cowboys and, at least Bert hoped, of Indians also.

"This is really the West, isn't it?" said Bert to his father, as they saw the wide, rolling fields on either side of the train.

"Yes, this is the West," was the answer.

"But where are the cowboys and the cows?" Nan asked.

"Oh, they don't come so close to the railroad," her father explained. "You'll see them when you get to the ranch."

Then the train reached the small station, as I have said. It seemed to be very lonesome. There were no other buildings near it—only a water tank, and there was not an Indian in sight. At first Bert thought there was not even a cowboy, but when he saw a man sitting on the seat of a wagon with some horses hitched in front—horses that had queer, rough marks on their flanks—Bert cried:

"Oh, say! I guess he's a cowboy!" and he pointed to the driver.

"He hasn't any cow!" exclaimed Flossie, and she wondered why the man in the wagon laughed.

"No, I haven't any cows with me," he said; "but if this is the Bobbsey family I can take you to a place where you will see lots of cattle."

"We are the Bobbseys," said the children's

father, walking over to the man in the wagon. "Are you from Three Star ranch?"

"That's where I'm from. I'm in charge, for the time being, but I can't stay much longer. You'll have to get another foreman. I got your letter, saying you were coming out, so I stayed to meet you. And now, if you're ready, I'll take you all out to Three Star."

"Is Three Star the name of a city?" asked Bert.

"No, it's the name of the ranch your mother owns, my boy," said the man, who gave his name as Dick Weston. "All the cattle are marked, or branded, with three stars—like the ponies there," and he pointed to the rough marks on the flanks of the team.

"As soon as I saw those marks I knew you must be a cowboy," said Bert. "You do ride a horse, don't you?"

"That's about all I do," said Foreman Weston, with a smile. "I don't often ride in a wagon, but I knew you'd need one to-day to get to the ranch. Now, if you're ready, we'll start."

The train had gone on, after leaving the

Bobbseys and their baggage. Into the wagon the twins were helped. Mr. and Mrs. Bobbsey took their seats, the driver called to the horses and away they trotted.

"Is Cowdon much of a town?" asked Mr. Bobbsey, as they drove along.

"No, not much more than you can see over there," and Dick Weston pointed with his whip to a few houses and a store or two on the prairie, about a mile from the railroad station. "We don't go through it to get to Three Star ranch. We turn off to the north," and he drove along the prairie road.

"Oh, look at that snake!" suddenly cried Bert, pointing to one that wiggled and twisted across the road.

"Yes, and you want to look out for those snakes," said the driver. "That's a rattler, and poisonous. Keep away from 'em!"

"Yes indeed they must!" said Mrs. Bobbsey. "Are there any other dangers out here?"

"Well, not many, no, ma'am. And rattlers aren't to be feared if you let 'em alone. Just keep clear of 'em. They'll run away from you rather than fight."

Up and down little, rolling hills went the wagon, drawing the Bobbsey twins. They dipped down into a hollow, and for a time nothing could be seen but green fields.

"Where are the cows?" asked Nan.

"And the cowboys?" Bert wanted to know.

"You'll see 'em soon," was the promise of the driver.

All of a sudden a great noise burst out. There was the shooting of pistols and loud shouts.

"Yi! Yi! Yip!" came in shrill cries.

"Woo! Wow!" sounded, as if in answer.

"Bang! Bang!" went the firearms.

"What is that?" cried Nan, holding her hands over her ears.

"Those are the cowboys," answered Dick Weston, with a smile. "That's their way of telling you they're glad to see you. Here we are at the ranch."

CHAPTER XVIII

A RUNAWAY PONY

SUDDENLY the noise of the shooting and shouting stopped. The children looked up toward the top of a little hill, for the sounds seemed to have come from the other side of that. As yet they had seen nothing that looked like a ranch, nor had they caught a glimpse of any cows or cowboys.

But, all at once Flossie cried:

"Oh, there they are! I see 'em!"

"So do I!" echoed Freddie.

And, with that, over the hill came racing about ten laughing, shouting and cheering men, each one waving his hat in one hand while the other held aloft something black, and from this black thing came spurts of smoke and banging noises.

"There are the cowboys! There are the

cowboys! I'm going to be one of them!" cried Bert.

"Yes, there are the cowboys sure enough!" said Mr. Bobbsey.

"Will they shoot us?" asked Flossie.

"No they won't shoot anybody!" said the driver with a laugh. "They only keep their revolvers—guns they call 'em—to drive the wolves away from the cattle. This is only their way of having fun. They'll soon stop."

"Oh, what fun to be a cowboy and shoot a pistol!" cried Bert, as he saw the prancing horses. "I'm going to be one."

"You'll have to grow up a little bigger," said Dick Weston; "though you're pretty good-sized now."

The Bobbsey twins and the Bobbsey grown-ups watched the cowboys as they rode up on their "ponies", as the horses were called.

"Hi, there!" called the leading cowboy. "Are the Bobbsey twins there in that outfit, Dick?"

"That's what!" answered the driver. "The Bobbsey twins are here! I've got all four of 'em!"

"Hurray! Hurray! Hurray!" cheered the cowboys.

"How did they know our names?" asked Nan of her mother, as the cowboys on their horses surrounded the wagon.

"Well, I had to write to tell the man in charge of the Three Star ranch that we were coming," answered Mrs. Bobbsey. "I mentioned that I had four little Bobbsey twins, and of course the cowboys remembered. They seem glad to see us."

And, indeed, it was a most hearty welcome that was given the Bobbsey family on their trip to the great West. Not only the lumbermen, but the men at the ranch were glad to see them.

"Are these the cowboys who work for you?" asked Mrs. Bobbsey of Dick Weston as the men on the ponies put up their pistols, placed their broad-brimmed hats on their heads and rode along beside the wagon.

"Well, you might say they work for you now, as you own this Three Star ranch," the foreman said. "Of course I hire the men, or rather, I did, but after I leave you'll have to get some one else to be foremen and hire the men. I only stayed until you got here. I have a big ranch of my own that another man and I bought. I'll have to go and look after that."

"I shall be sorry to see you go, Mr. Weston," said the children's mother. "Do you know where I can get another foreman?"

"Well, I'm sort of sorry to go myself, after I've seen these twins," replied the driver. "We don't very often see children out here. It's too lonesome for 'em. But I just have to go. As for another foreman, why, I guess you won't have any trouble picking one up. Any of the cowboys will act as foreman until you get a regular one."

"I am glad to know that," said Mrs. Bobbsey.

"Is that the ranch?" asked Bert as the party of cowboys, riding around the carriage, suddenly started off down a little hill, and Bert pointed to several buildings clustered together at the foot of the slope almost like the buildings at the lumber camp.

"Well, all this is Three Star ranch," answered the foreman, and he swept his arm in a big circle across the prairie fields. "But those are the ranch houses and corrrals."

"I don't see any cows," said Nan, and this seemed to puzzle her.

"The cattle are mostly out on the different fields, or 'ranges', as we call 'em, feeding," said Mr. Weston. "We drive them from place to place as they eat the grass. We don't generally keep many head of cattle right around the ranch buildings. We have a cow or two for milk, and maybe a calf or so."

"Oh, may I have a little calf?" cried Freddie. "If I'm going to be a cowboy I want a little calf."

"I guess we can get you one," said Mr. Weston, with a smile. "Well, here we are," he went on, as he drove the wagon up in front of a one-story red building, with a low, broad porch. "This is the main ranch house where your uncle used to live part of the time, Mrs. Bobbsey," he said. "I think you'll find it big enough for your family. We fixed it up as best we could when we heard you were coming."

"Oh, I'm sure you have made it just like a

home!" said Mrs. Bobbsey in delight, as she went into the house with her husband and the children. "Oh, how lovely!"

There were some bright-colored rugs on the floor, and in vases on the table and mantel were some prairie flowers. On the walls of the one big room, which seemed to take up most of the house, were oddly colored cow skins, mounted horns, and the furry pelt of some animal that Bert thought was a wolf.

"I'm sure we shall like it here," said Mrs. Bobbsey. "I am glad we came to Three Star ranch."

"So'm I!" said Bert.

"And can I get an Indian doll?" asked Nan.

"Well, there are a few Indians around here," said the foreman slowly. "They come to the ranch now and then to get something to eat, or trade a pony. I don't know that I've ever seen any of 'em with a doll, though maybe they do have some."

"Will any Indian come soon?" Nan wanted to know.

"I hope they do—real wild ones!" cried Bert.

"We don't have that kind here," said the foreman. "All the Indians around here are tame. And I can't say when they will come."

"Well, anyhow, there's cowboys," said Bert hopefully.

The baggage was brought in and then the foreman said to Mr. Bobbsey:

"When do you want to eat?"

"Right now!" exclaimed Bert, before any one else had a chance to speak.

"I thought so!" laughed the foreman. "Tell Sing Foo to rustle in the grub," he went on to one of the cowboys on the outside porch.

"Oh, do you have a Chinese laundryman for a cook?" asked Nan, as she heard the name.

"Well, I guess Sing Foo can wash, bake, iron, mend clothes, or do anything around the ranch except ride a cow pony or brand a steer," said Dick Weston. "He draws the line on that. But he surely is a good cook with the grub," said the foreman.

"I don't want any grub," put in Freddie anxiously. "I want something to eat."

"Excuse me, little man. I guess I oughtn't to use slang before you." said the foreman.

"When I say 'grub' I mean something to eat. And here comes Sing Foo with it now!"

As he spoke a smiling Chinese, dressed jus as the Bobbsey twins had seen them in pictures, with his shirt outside his trousers, came shuffling along, carrying big trays from which came delicious appetizing odors.

"Dlinna all leddy!" said Sing Foo. "All leddy numbla one top side pletty quick."

"He means dinner is all ready and that everything is cooked just right and in a hurry," explained the foreman. "He can't say any words well that have the letter "r" in 'em," he went on in a whisper.

The Chinese was busy setting the table, and the Bobbseys soon sat down to a fine meal. Dick Weston ate with them and explained things about the ranch to Mr. and Mrs. Bobbsey. The twins were too busy looking around the room and out of the windows through which now and then they could see some of the cowboys, to pay much attention to the talk of the grown-ups.

As Mr. Weston had said, he was going to give up being foreman of Three Star ranch to take charge of a place he and another man had bought. He was only staying until Mrs. Bobbsey could come and take charge of her property. But Mr. Weston said she would have no trouble, with her husband and the cowboys to help her."

"But I don't know anything about cows or cowboys," said Mr. Bobbsey. "When it comes to lumber and trees I'm all right. But I'll be of no use here. We must get another foreman, my dear," he said to his wife.

"Yes, undoubtedly," she agreed. "Oh, look at the children," she went on, pointing out of the window. Bert and Nan and Flossie and Freddie had left the table after the meal, and were now out near one of the cattle yards, or corrals, standing beside a little cart to which a pony was hitched.

"They mustn't get into that pony cart," said Mrs. Bobbsey, for she saw Bert lifting Freddie up into the small wagon, while Nan was doing the same for Flossie.

"They won't hurt it, ma'am," said the foreman. "I brought that pony cart around on purpose, so you could give it to the children.

It's been here some time, but as there weren't any children it hasn't been used much. The boys got the cart out and mended it when they heard the Bobbsey twins were coming."

"That is very kind of them, I'm sure," said Mr. Bobbsey. "Is the pony safe to drive?"

"Oh, yes, your older boy or girl can manage him all right. Look, they're all in now. We can go out and I'll tell them what to do."

But before Mr. and Mrs. Bobbsey and the foreman could reach the pony cart, in which the Bobbsey twins were now seated, something happened. There was the report of a shot, and a moment later the pony started off at a fast gallop, dragging the cart and the children after him.

"Oh, he's running away!" cried Mrs. Bobbsey. "Stop the runaway pony!"

CHAPTER XIX

THE WILD STEER

PONIES can not run as fast as can horses, not being as large. But the pony drawing the small cart into which the Bobbsey twins had climbed seemed to go very swiftly indeed. Before Mr. and Mrs. Bobbsey and Dick Weston, the foreman, could hurry outside the ranch house, the pony and cart were quite a distance down the road which led over the prairies to the distant cattle ranges.

"Oh, the children! What will happen to them?" cried Mrs. Bobbsey, as she saw the twins being carried away.

"Perhaps Bert can get hold of the reins and stop the pony," said Mr. Bobbsey, as he hurried along with his wife.

"If he can do that they'll be all right," said the foreman. "The pony is a good one, and I never knew him to run away before. That shot must have frightened him."

But whatever had caused the pony to run away, the little horse certainly was going fast. Sitting in the cart, the Bobbsey twins had been too frightened at first to know what was going on. As soon as Bert and Nan had followed Flossie and Freddie up into the small cart the shot had sounded and away the pony galloped, the reins almost slipping over the dashboard.

"Oh, Bert!" cried Nan, grasping Flossie and Freddie around their waists so the small twins would not fall out, "what shall we do?"

Bert did not answer just then. For one thing he had to hold on to the side of the cart so he would not be jostled out. And another reason he did not answer Nan was because he was trying to think what was the best thing to do.

He looked ahead down the ranch road, and did not see anything into which the pony might crash, and so hurt them all. The road was clear. Behind him Bert could hear his mother, his father, and the foreman shouting. Bert hoped some of the cowboys might be there also, and that they would run after and stop the pony. But when he looked back he did not see any of the big, jolly, rough men on their speedy little cow ponies.

Bert saw his father and mother, and also Mr. Weston running after the pony cart, and Bert wondered why the foreman did not get on his horse and gallop down the road. Afterward Bert learned that the foreman had loaned his horse to another cowboy, who had ridden on it to a distant part of the ranch. And none of the cowboys was near by when the pony ran away.

"Oh, Bert! what will happen?" asked Nan, still holding Flossie and Freddie to keep them from falling out of the swaying cart. "What are we going to do?"

"I'm going to try to stop this pony!" answered Bert. He saw where the reins had nearly slipped over the dashboard. The reins were buckled together, and the loop had caught on one of the ends of the nickle-plated rail on top of the dashboard. Bert leaned forward to get hold of the reins, so he might bring the pony to a stop, but the little horse gave a sudden jump just then, as a bird flew in front of him. The reins slipped down and dragged along the ground. Bert could not reach them, and the pony seemed to go faster than ever.

"Oh, dear!" cried Nan. "We'll all be hurt!"

Flossie and Freddie were very much frightened, and clung closely to Sister Nan.

But presently Freddie plucked up courage and then grew excited, and after a minute or two he called out:

"We're havin' a fast ride, we are!"

"Too fast!" exclaimed Bert. "But maybe he'll get tired pretty soon and stop!"

However, the pony did not seem to be going to stop very soon. On and on he ran, with Mr. and Mrs. Bobbsey and the ranch foreman being left farther and farther behind.

Suddenly, along a side path that joined the main road on which the pony was running away, appeared the figure of a man on a horse. He was trotting along slowly, at first, but as soon as he caught sight of the pony cart and the children in it, this man made his horse go much faster.

"Sit still! Sit still! I'll stop your pony for you!" called the man.

Bert and Nan heard. They looked up and saw the stranger waving his hand to them. He was guiding his galloping horse so as to cut across in front of their trotting pony.

In a few moments the man on the big horse was closer. Then began a race between the horse and the pony, and because the horse was bigger and had longer legs it won. The man galloped up beside the pony cart, leaped down from his saddle and caught the pony by the bridle. It was easy for the man to halt the little horse, and bring the pony to a stop.

"There you are, children!" said the man. "Not hurt, I hope?"

"No, sir," answered Bert. "We're all right."

"Thank you," added Nan, for she noticed that Bert was forgetting this very important part.

"Oh, yes. Thank you!" said Bert.

"You are quite welcome," the man said. "But you shouldn't try to make your pony go so fast."

"We didn't make him go fast," replied Bert.

"We'd just got in the cart, to see if we would all fit, and somebody shot a gun and the pony ran away."

"Did he run far?" asked the man.

"Yes, he gave us a long ride," answered Freddie.

"Oh, it wasn't so very far," added Nan. "Though it seemed like a good way because we went so fast."

"We're from Three Star ranch," explained Bert.

"Oh, so you live on a ranch," said the man. "Well, I'm looking for a ranch myself."

"We don't exactly live on a ranch," went on Bert. "But it's my mother's, and we came out West to see it. Before that we were at a lumber camp."

"My! you are doing some traveling," exclaimed the man, who was rubbing the velvet nose of the pony. "Are these some of your friends coming?" he asked, looking down the road.

The Bobbsey twins turned and looked, and saw their father and mother and the foreman hurrying along. When the father and mother saw that the pony had been stopped and that the children were safe, they were no longer frightened.

"He stopped the pony for us," explained Bert, pointing to the stranger who had mounted his horse as Mr. Weston took hold of the pony's bridle, so it would not try to run away again.

"You appeared just in time," said Mr. Bobbsey to the strange man. "The children might have been hurt, only for you."

"Well, I'm glad I could stop the runaway," was the answer. "They said they lived on a ranch around here."

"Yes, the Three Star," said Mr. Weston. "You look like a cattleman yourself," he added.

"I am," said the man. "My name is Charles Dayton, and I am looking for a place to work. I was foreman at the Bar X ranch until that outfit was sold. I've been looking for a place ever since."

"The Bar X!" cried Mr. Weston. "I know some of the cowboys over there. And so you are looking for a place as foreman. Why, this is strange. Mrs. Bobbsey here, the owner of

Three Star, is looking for a foreman. I'm going to leave."

"Well, I would be very glad to work for Mrs. Bobbsey at Three Star," said Mr. Dayton.

"Are you any relation to a Bill Dayton?" asked Mr. Bobbsey, while Bert and Nan listened for the answer. Flossie and Freddie were out of the cart now, gathering prairie flowers, and did not pay much attention to the talk.

"Bill Dayton is my brother," answered Charles Dayton. "But I did not know he was around here. The last I heard of him he was in the lumber business."

"And he is yet!" exclaimed Mrs. Bobbsey. "He is foreman of a lumber tract my uncle left me."

"And if you are as good a cattleman as your brother is a lumberman I think we can find a place for you at Three Star," said Mr. Bobbsey.

"I can tell you Mr. Dayton is a good cattleman," said Mr. Weston. "He had to be, to act as foreman at Bar X ranch. You won't make any mistake in hiring him."

"Will you come to us?" asked Mr. Bobbsey, who seemed to have taken as much of a liking to the newcomer as had the children.

"Well, I'm looking for a place," was the answer, "and I'll do my best to suit you. It's queer, though, that you know my brother Bill."

"He mentioned you," said Mr. Bobbsey, "but he said he had lost track of you."

"Yes, we don't write to each other very often. Both of us have been traveling around a lot. But now, if I settle down, I'll send Bill a letter and tell him where I am."

There was room for Mrs. Bobbsey in the pony cart, and she rode back with the children. There seemed to be no danger now, for the little horse had quieted down.

"He hadn't been out of the stable for some time, and that's what made him so frisky," said the foreman, who was soon going to leave Three Star. "He won't run away again."

And Toby, which was the name of the pony, never did. Bert and Nan drove him often after that, and there never was a bit of trouble. Even Freddie and Flossie were allowed to drive, when Bert or Nan sat on the seat near them, in case of accident.

Mr. Charles Dayton soon proved that he was a good cattleman, and he was made foreman of Three Star ranch after Dick Weston left. The cowboys seemed to like their new foreman.

"And, now that you are one of us here," said Mrs. Bobbsey to her new foreman, "don't forget to write and let your brother know where you are."

"I'll do that!" promised the cattleman.

Busy and happy days on the ranch followed. While Mr. and Mrs. Bobbsey looked after the new business of raising and selling cattle, the Bobbsey twins had good times. The new foreman and the cowboys were very fond of the children, and were with them as much as they could be during the day. They took them on little picnics and excursions, and two small ponies were trained so Bert and Nan could ride them. As for Flossie and Freddie, they had to ride in the cart. Freddie wanted to be a cowboy, and straddle a pony as Bert did, but his mother thought him too small. But Freddie and Flossie had good times in the cart, so they did not miss saddle rides.

Bert and Nan were very fond of their ponies The little horses soon grew very tame and gentle, though Bert and his sister did not go very far away from the main buildings unless some of the cowboys were with them.

One afternoon, when they had been on the ranch about a month, and were liking it more and more every day, Bert and Nan asked their mother if they could ride on their ponies across the fields to gather a new kind of wild flower a cowboy had told them about.

"Yes, you may go," Mrs. Bobbsey said. "But be careful, and do not ride too far. Be home in time for supper."

"We will," promised Bert.

He and Nan set off. It was pleasant riding over the green prairie. Now and then the children saw little prairie dogs scurrying in and out of their burrows. And once they saw a rattlesnake. But the serpent crawled quickly out of the way, and Bert and Nan did not stop to see where it went. They hurried on.

They reached the little hollow in the hills

where the red flowers grew, and, getting out of their saddles, began to pick some.

"They'll make a lovely bouquet for the living room," said Nan.

"Yes, but I guess we have enough," said Bert. "I don't want to stay here too long. Mr. Dayton promised to show me how to throw a lasso to-day, and I've got to learn; that is, if I'm going to be a cowboy."

"All right," agreed Nan. "We'll go in a minute. I want to get just a few more flowers." She was gathering another handful of the red blossoms when suddenly she looked up, and something she saw on top of a little hill caused her to cry:

"Oh, Bert, look! Look! What's that?"

Bert glanced up. He saw a wild steer looking at him and his sister. The big animal was lashing his tail from side to side and pawing the earth with one hoof. Suddenly it gave a loud bellow and rushed down the slope.

CHAPTER XX

THE ROUND-UP

BERT and Nan were really too frightened to know what to do. If they had been more used to the ways of the West, and had known more about cattle and ranches, they would have at once run for their ponies and have got on the backs of the little animals. Cattle in the West are so used to seeing men on horse back that sometimes if they see them on foot on the wide prairie, the cattle chase the men, thinking they are a strange enemy.

Perhaps it was this way with the wild steer. At any rate, seeing Bert and Nan gathering flowers down in the hollow of the hills, the steer, with loud bellows, started down toward them. The two ponies were eating grass near by, and Bert and Nan could easily have reached their pets if they had thought of it.

But they were so frightened that they could

not think. As for the ponies, those little horses merely looked up. They saw the steer, but, as they saw such animals every day, the ponies were not at all interested.

"Oh, Bert," cried Nan, "what shall we do?"

She had dropped her flowers and was running toward her brother.

"You get behind me!" cried Bert. "Maybe I can throw a stone at this steer!"

He, too, had dropped the red blossoms he had gathered, and was looking about for a stone. But he could not see any, and the wild steer was coming on down the slope. I do not mean that the steer was wild, like a wild lion or tiger, but that he was just excited by seeing two children off their ponies. If Bert and Nan had been in the saddles perhaps the steer never would have chased them.

But now with tail flapping in the air, and with angry shakes of his head, he was running toward them. Nan got behind her brother, and Bert stood ready to do what he could. The children did not realize how much danger they were in and they might have been hurt but for something that happened.

At first neither Bert nor Nan knew what this happening was. One moment they saw the wild steer racing toward them, and the next minute they saw the big animal, larger than a cow, tumbling down the hill head over heels. The steer seemed to have fallen, and a look toward the crest of the hill showed what had made him. For up at the top of the slope, sitting on his big horse, was the new foreman, Charley Dayton, and from his saddle horn a rope stretched out. The other end of the rope was around the steer's neck, and it was a pull on this rope that had caused the big beast to turn a somersault.

"Oh, he lassoed the steer! He lassoed him!" cried Bert, as he saw what had happened.

And that is just what the foreman had done. He had been out riding over the ranch, and had seen the lone steer on top of the hill which he knew led down into a hollow filled with red flowers.

"At first," said Mr. Dayton to Nan and Bert, telling them the story afterward, "I couldn't imagine why the steer was acting so queerly. I thought may be he didn't like the red flowers

So I rode up to see what the matter was. Then I saw you children down in the hollow and saw the steer rushing at you.

"There was only one thing I could do, and I did it. I didn't even stop to shout to you Bobbsey twins!" said the foreman. "I just swung my lasso and caught the steer before he caught you."

"You made him turn a somersault, didn't you?" said Nan, as she and Bert looked at the big beast which was now lying on the ground.

"Well, he sort of made himself do it," answered the foreman, with a laugh. "He was going so fast, and the lasso rope on his neck made him stop so quickly that he went head over heels. But you had better get into your saddles now, and I'll let this fellow up."

Mr. Dayton had twisted some coils of his rope around the steer's legs so the animal could not get up until the foreman was ready to let him. But as soon as Bert and Nan had gathered the flowers they had dropped, and had seated themselves in their saddles, and when the foreman had mounted his horse, he shook loose the coils of the rope, or lasso, and the steer scrambled to his feet.

"Will he chase us again?" asked Nan.

"No, I guess I taught him a lesson," answered Mr. Dayton.

The steer shook himself and looked at the three figures on the horse and ponies. He did not seem to want to chase anybody now, and after a shake or two of his head the steer walked away, up over the hill and across the prairie, to join the rest of the herd from which he had strayed.

"You want to be careful about getting off your ponies when you see a lone steer," the foreman told Bert and Nan. "Some animals think a person on foot is a new kind of creature and want to give chase right away. On a cattle ranch keep in the saddle as much as you can when you are among the steers."

Bert and his sister said they would do this, and then they rode home with the red flowers. Mr. and Mrs. Bobbsey thanked the foreman for again saving the children from harm.

Mr. Charles Dayton seemed to fit in well at Three Star ranch. He was as good a ranchman as his brother Bill was a lumberman. And, true to the promise he had given Mrs. Bobbsey, the ranch foreman wrote to Bill, giving the address of Three Star.

"I had a letter from Bill to-day, Mrs. Bobbsey," said the ranch foreman to the children's mother one afternoon.

"Did you? That's good!" she answered.

"And he says he'd like to see me," went on Mr. Charles Dayton. "He says he has something to tell me."

"Did he say what it was about?" asked Mrs. Bobbsey, while Bert and Nan stood near by. They were waiting for the foreman to saddle the ponies for them, as he always wanted to be sure the girths were made tight enough before the twins set out for a ride.

"No, Bill didn't say what it was he wanted to tell me," went on Charley. "And he writes rather queerly."

"Your brother seemed to me to be a bit odd," said Mrs. Bobbsey. "As if he had some sort of a secret."

"Oh, well, I guess he has had his troubles, the same as I have." said the ranch foreman.

"We were boys together, and we didn't have a very good time. I suppose it was as much our fault as any one's. But you don't think of that at the time. Well, I'll be glad to see Bill again, but I don't know when we'll get together. Are you waiting for me, Bobbsey twins?" he asked.

"Yes, if you please," answered Nan.

"We'd like our ponies," added Bert, "and you promised to show me some more how to lasso."

"And so I will!" promised the foreman. He had already given Bert a few lessons in casting the rope. Of course Bert could not use a lasso of the regulation size, so one of the cowboys had made him a little one. With this Bert did very well. Freddie also had to have one, but his was only a toy. Freddie wanted his father to call him "little cowboy" now, instead of "little fireman," and, to please Freddie, Mr. Bobbsey did so once in a while.

After Bert had been given a few more lessons in casting the lasso, the two older Bobbsey twins went for a ride on their ponies, while

Mrs. Bobbsey took Flossie and Freddie for a ride in the pony cart.

It was about a week after this that the Bobbsey twins were awakened one morning by a loud shouting outside the ranch house where they slept.

"What's the matter? Have the Indians come?" asked Bert, for some of the cowboys had said a few Indians from a neighboring reservation usually dropped in for a visit about this time of year.

"No, I don't see any Indians," answered Nan, who had looked out of a window, after hurriedly getting dressed. "But I see a lot of the cowboys."

"Oh, maybe they're going after the Indians!" exclaimed Bert. I'm going to ask mother if I can go along!"

"I want to go, too, and get an Indian doll!" exclaimed Nan.

But when they went out into the main room, where their father and mother were eating breakfast, and when the two Bobbsey twins had begged to be allowed to go with the cowboys to see the Indians, Mr. Bobbsey said:

"This hasn't anything to do with Indians, Bert."

"What's it all about then?" asked the boy.

"It's the round-up," answered his father. "The cowboys are getting ready for the half-yearly round-up, and that's what they're so excited about."

"Oh, may I see the round-up?" begged Bert.

"What is it?" asked Nan. "What's a round-up?"

Before Mr. Bobbsey could answer Mr. Dayton, the foreman, came hurrying into the room. He seemed quite excited.

"Excuse me for disturbing your breakfast," he said to Mr. and Mrs. Bobbsey. "But I have some news for you. Some Indians have run off part of your cattle!"

CHAPTER XXI

IN THE STORM

BERT BOBBSEY did not pay much attention to what the foreman said, except that one word "Indians."

"Oh, where are they?" cried the boy. "I want to see them!"

"And I'd like to see them myself!" exclaimed the foreman. "If I could find them I'd get back the Three Star cattle."

"Did Indians really take some of the steers?" asked Mrs. Bobbsey.

"Yes," answered the foreman, "they did. You know we are getting ready for the round-up. That is a time, twice a year, when we count the cattle, and sell what we don't want to keep," he explained, for he saw that Nan wanted to ask a question.

"Twice a year," went on the foreman, "once in the spring and again in the fall, we have what is called a round-up. That is we gather together all the cattle on the different parts of the ranch. Some herds have been left to themselves for a long time, and it may happen that cattle belonging to some other ranch-owner have got in with ours. We separate, or 'cut out,' as it is called, the strange cattle, give them to the cowboys who come for them, and look after our own. That is a round-up, and sometimes it lasts for a week or more. The cowboys take a 'chuck', or kitchen wagon with them, and they cook their meals out on the prairie."

"Oh, that's fun!" cried Bert. "Please, Daddy, mayn't I go on the round-up?"

"And have the Indians catch you?" asked his mother.

"Oh, there isn't any real danger from the Indians," said the foreman. "They are not the wild kind. Only, now and again, they run off a bunch of cattle from some herd that is far off from the main ranch. This is what has happened here."

"How did you find out about it?" asked Mr. Bobbsey.

"A cowboy from another ranch told me," answered the foreman. "Some of his cattle were taken and he followed along the trail the Indians left. He saw them, but could not catch them. But he saw some of the cattle that had strayed away from the band of Indians, and these steers were branded with our mark—the three stars."

"Well, maybe the poor Indians were hungry," said Mrs. Bobbsey. "And that is why they took some of our steers."

"Yes, I reckon that's what they'd say, anyhow," remarked the foreman. "But it won't do to let the redmen take cattle any time they feel like it. They have money, and can buy what they want. I wouldn't mind giving them a beef or two, but when it comes to taking part of a herd, it must be stopped."

"How can it be stopped?" asked Mr. Bobbsey.

"That's just what I came in to talk to you about," went on Mr. Dayton. "Shall I send some of the cowboys after the Indians to see if they can catch them, and get back our cattle?"

"I suppose you had better," Mr. Bobbsey

answered. "If we let this pass the Indians will think we do not care, and will take more steers next time. Yes, send the cowboys after the Indians."

"But let the Indians have a steer or two for food, if they need it," begged Mrs. Bobbsey, who had a kind heart even toward an Indian cattle thief, or "rustler", as they are called.

"Well, that can be done," agreed Mr. Dayton. "Then I'll send some of the cowboys on the round-up, and others after the Indians. They can work together, the two bands of cowboys."

"Oh, mayn't I come?" begged Bert. "I can throw a lasso pretty good now, and maybe I could rope an Indian."

"And maybe you could get me an Indian doll!" put in Nan.

"Oh, no! We couldn't think of letting you go, Bert," said Mr. Bobbsey. "The cowboys will be gone several nights, and will sleep out on the open prairie. When you get bigger you may go."

Bert looked so disappointed that the foreman said:

"I'll tell you what we can do. Toward the end of the round-up the boys drive the cattle into the corrals not far from here. The children can go over then and see how the cowboys cut out different steers, and how we send some of the cattle over to the railroad to be shipped back east. That will be seeing part of the round-up, anyhow."

And with this Bert had to be content. He and Nan, with Flossie and Freddie, watched the cowboys riding away on their ponies, shouting, laughing, waving their hats and firing their revolvers.

While the round-up was hard work for the cowboys, still they had exciting times at it and they always were glad when it came. The ranch seemed lonesome after the band of cowboys had ridden away, but Sing Foo, the Chinese cook, was left, and one or two of the older men to look after things around the buildings. Mr. Dayton also stayed to see about matters for Mrs. Bobbsey.

It was well on toward fall now, though the weather was still warm. The days spent by the Bobbsey twins in the great West had passed so quickly that the children could hardly believe it was almost time for them to go back to Lakeport.

"Can't we stay here all winter?" asked Bert. "If I'm going to be a cowboy I'd better stay on a ranch all winter."

"Oh, the winters here are very cold," his father said. "We had better go back to Lakeport for Christmas, anyhow," and he smiled at his wife.

"Maybe Santa Claus doesn't come out here so far," said Freddie.

"Then I don't want to stay," said Flossie. "I want to go where Santa Claus is for Christmas."

"I think, then, we'd better plan to go back home," said Mrs. Bobbsey.

It was rather lonesome at the ranch now, with so many of the cowboys away, but the children managed to have good times. The two smaller twins often went riding in the pony cart, while Bert and Nan liked saddle-riding best.

One day as Bert and his sister started off their mother said to them:

"Don't go too far now. I think there is going to be a storm."

"We won't go far!" Bert promised.

Now the two saddle ponies were feeling pretty frisky that day. They seemed to know cold weather was coming, when they would have to trot along at a lively pace to keep warm. And perhaps Nan and Bert, remembering that they were soon to leave the ranch, rode farther and faster than they meant to.

At any rate they went on and on, and pretty soon Nan said:

"We had better go back. We never came so far away before, all alone. And I think it's going to rain!"

"Yes, it does look so," admitted Bert. "And I guess we had better go back. I thought maybe I could see some of the cowboys coming home from the round-up, but I guess I can't."

The children turned their ponies about, and headed them for the ranch house. As they did so the rain drops began to fall, and they had not ridden a half mile more before the storm suddenly broke.

"Oh, look at the rain!" cried Nan.

"And *feel* it!" exclaimed Bert. "This is going to be a big storm! Let's put on our ponchos."

The children carried ponchos on their saddles. A poncho is a rubber blanket with a hole in the middle. To wear it you just put your head through the hole, the rubber comes down over your shoulders and you are kept quite dry, even in a hard storm.

Bert and Nan quickly put on their ponchos and then started their ponies again. The rain was now coming down so hard that the brother and sister could scarcely see where they were going.

"Are we headed right for the house?" asked Nan.

"I—I guess so," answered Bert. "But I'm not sure."

CHAPTER XXII

NEW NAMES

BERT and Nan rode on through the rain which seemed to come down harder and harder. Soon it grew so dark, because it was getting to be late afternoon and because of the rain clouds, that the children could not see in the least where they were going.

"Oh, Bert, maybe we are lost!" said Nan, with almost a sob as she guided her pony up beside that of her brother.

"Oh, I don't guess we are exactly *lost,*" he said. "The ponies know their way back to the ranch houses, even if we don't."

"Do you think so?" Nan asked.

"Yes, Mr. Dayton told me if ever I didn't know which way to go, just to let the reins rest loose on the horse's neck, and he'd take me home."

"We'll do that!" decided Nan.

But whether the ponies did not know their way, or whether the ranch buildings were farther off than either Bert or Nan imagined, the children did not know. All they knew was that they were out in the rain, and they did not seem to be able to get to any shelter. There were no trees on the prairies about Three Star ranch, as there were in the woods at Lumberville.

"Oh, Bert, what shall we do?" cried Nan. "It's getting terribly dark and I'm afraid!"

Bert was a little afraid also, but he was not going to let his sister know that. He meant to be brave and look after her. They rode along a little farther, and suddenly Nan cried:

"Oh, Bert! Look! Indians!"

Bert, who was riding along with his head bent low to keep the rain out of his face, glanced up through the gathering dusk. He saw, just ahead of him and coming toward him and his sister a line of men on horses. But Bert either looked more closely than did his sister or else he knew more about Indians. For after a second glance he cried:

"They aren't Indians! They're cowboys!

Hello, there!" cried the boy. "Will you please show us the way to the house on Three Star ranch?"

Some of the leading cowboys pulled up their horses, and stopped on hearing this call. They peered through the rain and darkness and saw the two children on ponies.

"Who's asking for Three Star ranch?" cried one cowboy.

"We are!" Bert answered. "We're the Bobbsey twins!"

"Oh, ho! I thought so!" came back the answer. "Well, don't worry! We'll take you home all right!"

With that some of the cowboys (and they really were that and not Indians) rode closer to Nan and Bert. And as soon as Bert caught a glimpse of the faces of some of the men he cried:

"Why, you belong to Three Star!"

"Sure!" answered one, named Pete Baldwin. "We're part of the Three Star outfit coming back from the round-up. But where are you two youngsters going?"

"We came out for a ride," answered Bert

"but it started to rain, and we want to go home."

"Well, you won't get home the way you are going," said Pete. "You were traveling right away from home when we met you. Turn your ponies around, and head them the other way. We'll ride back with you."

Bert and Nan were glad enough to do this.

"It's a good thing we met you," said Bert, as he rode beside Pete Baldwin. "And did you catch the Indians?"

"Yes, we found them, and got back your mother's cattle—all except one or two we gave them."

"And is the round-up all over?" asked Bert.

"Yes, except for some cattle a few of the boys will drive in to-morrow or next day," the cowboy answered. "You can see 'em then. It's a good thing you youngsters had those rubber ponchos, or you'd be soaked through."

The cowboys each had on one of these rubber blankets, and they did not mind the rain. Some of them even sang as their horses plodded through the wet.

Bert and Nan were no longer afraid, and in

about half an hour they rode with their cowboy friends into the cluster of ranch buildings.

"Oh, my poor, dear children! where have you been?" cried Mrs. Bobbsey. "Daddy and Mr. Dayton were just going to start hunting for you! What happened?"

"We got lost in the rain, but the cowboys found us," said Bert.

"And first I thought they were Indians," added Nan, as she shook the water from her hair.

"Well, it's a good thing they did find you," said Mr. Bobbsey.

The two Bobbsey twins were given some warm milk to drink, and soon they were telling Flossie and Freddie about their ride in the rain.

"I wish I could see an Indian," sighed Freddie.

"All I want now is an Indian doll," said Nan.

Two days later the cowboys came riding in with a bunch of cattle which they had rounded-up and cut out from a larger herd. These steers were to be shipped away, but, for a time, were kept in a corral, or fenced-in pen, near the ranch buildings. There Bert and the other children went to look at the big beasts, and the Bobbsey twins watched the cowboys at work.

It was about a week after Bert and Nan had been lost in the rain that Mrs. Bobbsey met the foreman, Charles Dayton on the porch of the ranch house one day.

"Oh, Mr. Dayton!" called the children's mother, "I have had a letter from your brother Bill, who has charge of my lumber tract. He is coming on here."

"Bill is coming here?" exclaimed the cattle-man in great surprise. "Well, I'm right happy to hear that. I'll be glad to see him. Haven't seen him for several years. Is he coming here just to see me?"

"No," answered Mrs. Bobbsey, "he is coming here to see Mr. Bobbsey and myself about some lumber business. After we left your brother found there were some papers I had not signed, so, instead of my going back to Lumberville, I asked your brother to come here. I can sign the papers here as well as there, and this will give you two brothers a chance to meet."

"I am glad of that!" exclaimed the cattleman. "I suppose Bill and I are going to be kept pretty busy—he among the trees and I among the cattle—so we might not get a chance to meet for a long time. only for this."

"That's what I thought," said Mrs. Bobbsey, while Bert and Nan listened to the talk. "Well, your brother will be here next week."

"Oh, I'll be glad to see him!" exclaimed Bert.

"So will I!" echoed Nan. "I like our lumberman."

During the week that followed the Bobbsey twins had good times at Three Star ranch. The weather was fine, but getting colder, and Mr. and Mrs. Bobbsey began to think of packing to go home. They would do this, they said, as soon as they had signed the papers Bill Dayton was bringing to them.

And one day, when the wagon had been sent to the same station at which the Bobbseys left the train some months before, the ranch foreman came into the room where Mr. and

Mrs. Bobbsey were talking with the children and said:

"He's here!"

"Who?" asked Bert's father.

"My brother Bill! He just arrived! My, but he has changed!"

"And I suppose he said the same thing about you," laughed Mrs. Bobbsey.

"Yes, he did," admitted the ranch foreman. "It's been a good while since we were boys together. Much has happened since then."

Bill Dayton came in to see Mrs. Bobbsey. The two brothers looked very much alike when they were together, though Bill was younger. They appeared very glad to see one another.

Bill Dayton had brought quite a bundle of papers for Mr. and Mrs. Bobbsey to sign in connection with the timber business, and it took two days to finish the work. During that time the Bobbsey twins had fun in a number of ways, from riding on ponies and in the cart, to watching the cowboys.

One day when Nan and Bert were putting their ponies in the stable after a ride, they saw the two Dayton brothers talking together near the barn. Without meaning to listen, the Bobbsey twins could not help hearing what was said.

"Don't you think we ought to tell the boss?" asked the ranch foreman of his brother, the timber foreman.

"You mean tell Mr. Bobbsey?" asked Bill Dayton.

"Yes, tell Mrs. Bobbsey—she's the boss as far as we are concerned. We ought to tell them that our name isn't Dayton—or at least that that isn't the only name we have. They've been so good to us that we ought to tell them the truth," answered Charles.

"I suppose we ought," agreed Bill. "We'll do it!"

And then they walked away, not having noticed Bert or Nan.

The two Bobbsey twins looked at one another.

"I wonder what they meant?" asked Nan.

"I don't know," answered her brother. "We'd better tell daddy or mother."

A little later that day Bert spoke to his father, asking:

"Daddy, can a man have two names?"

"Two names? Yes, of course. His first name and his last name."

"No, I mean can he have two last names?" went on Bert.

"Not generally," Mr. Bobbsey said. "I think it would be queer for a man to have two last names."

"Well, the two foremen have two last names," said Bert. "Haven't they, Nan?"

"What do you mean?" asked their father.

Then Bert and Nan told of having overheard Bill and Charles talking about the need for telling Mr. and Mrs. Bobbsey the truth about their name.

"What do you suppose this means?" asked Mr. Bobbsey of his wife.

"I don't know," she replied. "But you remember we did think there was something queer about Bill Dayton at the lumber camp."

"I know we did. I think I'll have a talk with the two foremen," Mr. Bobbsey went on. "Maybe they would like to tell us something, but feel a little nervous over it. I'll just ask them a few questions."

And later, when Mr. Bobbsey did this, speaking of what Nan and Bert had overheard, Bill Dayton said:

"Yes, Mr. Bobbsey, we have a secret to tell you. We were going to some time ago, but we couldn't make up our minds to it. Now we are glad Nan and Bert heard what we said. I'm going to tell you all about it."

"You children had better run into the house," said Mr. Bobbsey to Nan and Bert, who stood near by.

"Oh, let them stay," said the ranch foreman. "It isn't anything they shouldn't hear, and it may be a lesson to them. To go to the very bottom, Mr. Bobbsey, Dayton isn't our name at all."

"What is, then?" asked Mr. Bobbsey.

"Hickson," was the unexpected answer. "We are Bill and Charley Hickson. We took the name of Dayton when we ran away from home, as that was our mother's name before she was married. And we have been called Bill and Charley Dayton ever since. But Hickson is our real name."

Bert and Nan looked at one another. Then

felt that they were on the edge of a strange secret.

"Bill and Charley Hickson!" exclaimed Nan.

"Oh, is your father's name Hiram?" Bert asked excitedly.

"Hiram? Of course it is!" cried Bill. "Hiram Hickson is the name of our father!"

"Hurray!" shouted Bert.

"Oh, oh!" squealed Nan.

"Then we've found you!" yelled both together.

"Found us?" echoed Bill. "Why, we weren't lost! That is, we—" he stopped and looked at his brother.

"There seems to be more of a mystery here," said Charley Hickson to give him his right name. "Do you know what it is?" he asked Mr. Bobbsey.

"Oh, let me tell him!" cried Bert.

"And I want to help!" added Nan.

"We know where your father is!" went on Bert eagerly.

"His name is Hiram Hickson!" broke in Nan.

"And he works in our father's lumberyard," added Bert.

"He said he had two boys who—who went away from home," said Nan, not liking to use the words "ran away."

"And the boys names were Charley and Bill," went on Bert. "He said he wished he could find you, and we said, when we started away from home, that maybe we could help. But I didn't ever think we could."

"I didn't either," said Nan.

"Well, you seem to have found us all right," said Bill Dayton Hickson, to give him his complete name. "Of course I'm not sure this Hiram Hickson who works in your lumberyard is the same Hiram Hickson who is our father," he added to Mr. Bobbsey.

"I believe he is," answered Mr. Bobbsey. "Three such names could hardly be alike unless the persons were the same. But I'll write to him and find out."

"And tell him we are sorry we ran away from home," added Charles. "We haven't had very good luck since—at least, not until we met the Bobbsey twins," he went on. "We were two foolish boys, and we ran away after a quarrel."

"Your father says it was largely his fault," said Mrs. Bobbsey, who had come to join in the talk. "I think you had all better forgive each other and start all over again," she added.

"That's what we'll do!" exclaimed Bill.

It was not long before a letter came from Mr. Hickson of Lakeport, saying he was sure the ranch and lumber foremen were his two missing boys. Mr. Bobbsey sent the old man money to come out to the ranch, where Bill and his brother were still staying. And on the day when Hiram Hickson was to arrive the Bobbsey twins were very much excited indeed.

"Maybe, after all, these won't be his boys," said Nan.

"Oh, I guess they will," declared Bert.

And, surely enough, when Hiram Hickson met the two foremen he held out his hands to them and cried:

"My two boys! My lost boys! Grown to be men! Oh, I'm so glad I have found you again!"

And then the Bobbseys and the cowboys who had witnessed the happy reunion went away and left the father and sons together.

So everything turned out as Bert and Nan hoped it would, after they had heard the two foremen speaking of their new name. And, in a way, the Bobbsey twins had helped bring this happy time about. If they had not gone to the railroad accident, if they had not heard Hiram Hickson tell about his long-missing sons, and if they had not heard the cowboy and the lumberman talking together, perhaps the little family would not have been so happily brought together.

Mr. Hickson and his sons told each other their stories. As the old man had said, there had been a quarrel at home, and his two sons, then boys, had been hot-headed and had run away. They traveled together for a time, and then separated. They did not want to go back home.

As the years went on, the two brothers saw each other once in a while, and then for many months they would neither see nor hear from each other. They kept the name Dayton, which they had taken after leaving their father. As for Mr. Hickson, at first he did not try to find his sons, but after his anger died away he felt lonely and wanted them back. He felt that it was because of his queerness that they had gone away.

But, though he searched, he could not find them.

"And I might never have found you if I hadn't been in the train wreck and met the Bobbsey twins," said Mr. Hickson. "Coming to Lakeport was the best thing I ever did."

"How's everything back in Lakeport?" asked Bert of Mr. Hickson, after the first greetings between father and sons were over.

"Oh, just about the same," was the answer. "We haven't had any more train wrecks, thank goodness."

"But we were in one!" exclaimed Freddie.

"So I heard. Well, I'm glad you weren't hurt. But I must begin to think of getting back to your lumberyard, I guess, Mr. Bobbsey."

"No, you're going to live with us," declared Charley. "Part of the time you can spend on

Three Star ranch with me, and the rest of the time you can live with Bill in the woods."

"Well, that will suit me all right," said Mr. Hickson, and so it was arranged. He was to spend the winter on the ranch, where he would help his son with Mrs. Bobbsey's cattle. Bill Hickson went back to the lumber camp, and a few days later the Bobbsey twins left for home.

Nan had her wish in getting an Indian doll. One day, just before they were to leave the ranch, a traveling band of Indians stopped to buy some cattle. The Indian women had pappooses, and some of the Indian children had queer dolls, made of pieces of wood with clothes of bark and skin. Mr. Bobbsey bought four of the dolls, one each for Nan and Flossie, and two for Nan's girl friends at home. For Bert and Freddie were purchased some bows and arrows and some Indian moccasins, or slippers, and head-dresses of feathers. So, after all, the Bobbsey twins really saw some Indians.

"Good-bye, Bobbsey twins!" cried all the cowboys, and they fired their revolvers in the air. The Bobbseys were seated in the wagon their baggage around them, ready to go to the station at Cowdon to take the train for the return to Lakeport. "Come and see us again!" yelled the cowboys.

"We will!" shouted Nan and Bert and Flossie and Freddie.

They were driven over the prairie to the railroad station, looking back now and then to see the shouting, waving cowboys and Charles Hickson and his father. The Bobbsey twins left happy hearts behind them.

They wondered if ever again they would have as wonderful a vacation. Of course they were going to, and very soon too. The story will be told in "The Bobbsey Twins at Cedar Camp."

And now, as they are on their homeward way, back to Dinah and Sam, back to Snoop and Snap, we will take leave of the Bobbsey twins.

THE END